PISSANT

AND

CINDERELLA

THE FAIRY TALE THAT WASN'T

by

Linda Kay Simmons

Pissant and Cinderella by Linda Kay Simmons

Published by Linda Kay Simmons

www.Facebook.com/LindaKaySimmonsAuthor

Pissant and Cinderella is a fictional memoir based on events relayed to the author by the people who inspired the two main characters, now deceased. This novel contains fictionalized scenes, composite and representative characters, and author-imagined dialogue. The content of *Pissant and Cinderella* does not reflect or represent the views of the people on whom the characters are based. It is the author's intent to give one possible voice to the title characters' inspirations. May they rest in peace.

ISBN 978-0-578-93653-6

Cover Design by Next Generation Designs

Praise for *Pissant and Cinderella*

There are times when Ms. Simmons' striking new novel, *Pissant and Cinderella*, hits notes that are almost too real, but her brisk, honest, and unique examination of a problem affecting many is based on a reality that many know to be true. Survivors of domestic abuse may have trouble reading a few portions, but my guess is that they will enthusiastically recommend it to others. ~**Dan Smith**, Hall of Fame Journalist and Author

The author handles a sensitive and dark subject with grace and thoughtful care. Given the manner in which Ms. Simmons writes, you will feel a personal connection to all of the characters and won't want to put this book down until you read the final words. ~**Lori Webber**, Former Clinical Researcher at Wake Forest School of Medicine

Linda Kay Simmons' *Pissant and Cinderella* is the story of a family in crisis. It had me opening and closing the book as I struggled with their lives, realizing that my struggles as an onlooker were nothing compared to theirs. It's a skillfully written book that will capture your emotions while bringing a disturbing reality into sharp focus. This story will resonate with too many of us, but its value lies in shedding light on a dark subject that deserves an avalanche of enlightenment. ~**Ginny Brock**, Author of upcoming *The Writers Cottage* and more

Pissant and Cinderella is another beautifully written page-turner from this compelling author with a provocative, gripping plot that is believable yet unbelievable. Her characters always have challenges, but Pissant had to endure unimaginable cruelty. This is a recommended read. ~**Cheryl Crouse**, Special Ed Teacher, Volunteer

A painfully honest study of incest and child molestation, not for the faint of heart. Simmons dares to expose family secrets most of us want to keep hidden. Until we can't. ~**Betsy Ashton**, author of *Eyes Without A Face*, *Unintended Consequences*, *Mad Max Mysteries,* and more

This book regarding children raised in an abusive home is a must-read from Linda Kay Simmons. My psychiatric patients and many of the CASA children I worked with came from abusive situations. Hopefully, readers in trauma will realize that assistance is available to help cope with torturous memories and addictions so as not to inflict further damage upon themselves or their offspring. Read this book and please consider being a court advocate for children: Casaprogram.org/volunteer. ~**June Kingan**, Retired Psychiatric Nurse and CASA Volunteer

Stirring and heartbreaking, yet hopeful and tender, *Pissant and Cinderella* is a rare find. I was drawn into the story from the start and impressed with how the author handled potentially horrific topics with such a light touch. She deftly provides enough information to paint a scene without hitting readers over the head with every sordid detail. Highly recommended. ~**Anne McAneny**, Author and Editor

This author never fails to entertain and surprise. *Pissant and Cinderella* tells the story of a dysfunctional family whose matriarch has the appearance of helping others but ignores the strife in her own home. Ms. Simmons has written a real page-turner. ~**Kathy Ann Petroski**

Pissant and Cinderella will make you think long after you finish reading. While you may not personally relate to the abuses Linda Kay Simmons writes about, you more than likely know someone who silently suffered through a similar home life and suffers still. ~**Jo Anne Haymore**, Holistic Life Coach

Table of Contents

Part Two

PISSANT

AND

CINDERELLA

THE FAIRY TALE THAT WASN'T

PART ONE

The butterfly counts not months,

but moments,

and has time enough.

~ Rabindranath Tagore

CHAPTER ONE

Bastard Boy

I scoop the last bean and final spoonful of mashed potatoes off my plate and into my mouth. I eat every bite because sometimes we don't get dinner, and I go to bed hungry. My older siblings tell me it wasn't always this way, not when Father was alive, but I never knew him. He died years before I was born. I'm the youngest of five.

Mama is beautiful, with red hair and twinkly blue eyes, except when she is worn-out tired. She cleans other people's houses and occasionally takes me with her to do odd jobs. I'm five and too young to go to school, so I don't mind much. Sometimes it's even fun, especially at the pharmacist's house. The cowlick in his hair loops up just like mine, and the divot in his chin— that's what he calls it, anyway—goes deep, same as mine.

When it's just the three of us in his big house, he and Mama laugh. He pats my head and lets me watch the television while they have "a little nip of gin." But one day last week, his wife came home, slapped Mama right across the face, and called her a floozie. All the while, the pharmacist did nothing but watch. Right after, Mama grabbed me by the hand, and we got away from there. With her face bright red, Mama cried the whole way home.

Mama doesn't clean that man's house anymore, but she has other customers. When I go to their places, I play with my toy trucks or help match the socks in the laundry. The wives usually pay Mama, but the husbands drop by our house about once a week with envelopes for Mama's rainy-day fund.

A loud knock at the door startles all of us. Mama's face goes pale as she rises from the table to see who it is. After she opens the door, three men enter the foyer just far enough for us to see them. My oldest sister, Adrian, whispers that it's the mayor, the pharmacist, and the schoolmaster—three very important people in our small Southern town.

"What do they want with Mama?" she asks no one in particular.

"Mama cleans their houses," I say.

While Mama and the men mumble in the foyer, my brothers and I have a food fight with the leftover cornbread. It's so rare for there to be leftovers that I feel guilty for wasting it, but I play along anyway. Just as my other sister joins in by dipping two fingers in her milk and casting droplets at my oldest brother, the men enter the dining room. We all sit up straight, staying still as statues, but I can feel Adrian's leg shaking next to mine.

"Get the Bastard Boy now," the schoolmaster says. "It's time to go."

I stare at my empty plate, but I can see my brother across from me, quaking with fear. He has lost all interest in his cornbread and beans.

With no warning, I am grabbed gruffly by the collar and lifted from the table, my feet barely able to touch the floor.

I never get to say goodbye to my family, and the last thing I hear as I'm marched out the door is the sound of my mother's sobs.

Schoolmaster drives me to an orphanage and drops me off with nary a word. I stay there until I'm seven. I do what is expected of me, and study hard, not wanting to be put on the streets as Headmistress often threatens. I refuse to think of Mama or the others. If she loved me, this wouldn't have happened.

A tall man with a craggy face shows up on an October Sunday afternoon desiring a companion for his son. I hear him tell Headmistress he no longer has a wife. I'm paraded in front of the man along with several other boys my age. I am the chosen one. I leave that afternoon in the man's big black car, with nothing but a paper bag containing my toothbrush and pajamas.

Once in the man's large home, I do what I'm told. What choice do I have? I don't like my stepbrother because he pulls cruel tricks on me. Thankfully, there is a library in the house. I find places to hide and read. Books are my companions as the years drag by.

I register for the draft as World War II rages on, but one leg is shorter than the other, so the military does not want me. I don't know what to do with my life, but I know I like science. I visit the University of Richmond on the recommendation of a former teacher and decide it's as good a place to be as any. I apply and am accepted for the fall term. I'm given a scholarship and take odd jobs to pay my way through.

Once I have my college degree, I do not look back. Better times must be coming now that the war is over.

CHAPTER TWO

Bastard Boy

Flowers bloom, their sweet fragrance filling the air, on a warm August day in 1948, when my eyes gradually focus on an attractive young woman strolling in the park with a book under her arm. Though I am usually shy with women, particularly ones I find beautiful, I walk toward her and speak first.

"I see you have a book, as do I. Perhaps we can sit on a bench together and read?" She smiles at me and says yes.

She is reading *The Second Sex* by Simone de Beauvoir, and I, George Orwell's *1984*. We talk a bit and agree to meet the following week at this very bench to exchange books.

Before long, I am under her spell and want to woo her and win her hand. But I have no money nor prospects for a suitable job,

5

even with a college degree. Every day I study the want ads looking for work.

Desperate to impress her, I steal flowers from the graves of the recently buried.

"Thank you so much for the bouquet," she says as we sit on our bench a week later. "It's very thoughtful of you, particularly after the day I've had at the law firm."

"Tell me about your day," I say.

"I've worked at the firm since I graduated from Randolph Macon. I do typing and filing, and it's tiresome. I have ambition, but I'm wasting my time, so I'm learning all I can about real estate and plan to sell it soon. I'll be very good at it too. Since the war's been over, everyone wants their own home."

"Why did you choose Randolph Macon if you didn't plan on teaching?"

"My father died when I was young, and Mother taught school. She passed away three years ago, leaving me a small inheritance, but it's about to run out. The way my father saw it, teaching and nursing were the only options for women. I don't do well with needles or blood, so I took the lesser of the evils."

"I believe you can sell real estate," I say. "And I'd like to help."

That very day, Anastasia allows me to walk her to the ladies' boarding house where she's lived for over a year. It isn't the best of places but neither is the room I rent by the week. I meet her when she gets off work at 5:00 p.m. Often, we stop for a bite to eat and a short walk before she retires for the night. The boarding house has strict rules.

It isn't long before we marry in this very park. I wear a blue suit, a lift in my shoe, and a carnation in my lapel. Anastasia walks down the makeshift grassy aisle with a limp in her step and a bouquet of yellow roses. We are both twenty-one.

CHAPTER THREE

Bastard Boy

It's a soggy day, and the leaves from the golden oaks fall like rain in the back of our soon-to-be home in Ashland. My wife, one of few local women in real estate, says it's good luck to buy a house on a day such as this. After a year of renting the upper level of an old Colonial and saving every penny, we're ready to buy our first home. I work at an insurance company, processing claims, and it's something I don't want to do for long.

It's not quite noon when Anastasia and I arrive at the three-story, white-framed house built in 1848, with four bedrooms, two baths, a formal dining room, and a living room with a large parlor. Sitting in the car, we reread the newspaper clipping written by the historical society, which claims that the attic was once used for the surgeries of wounded Confederate soldiers.

Several of the upper windows have shutters, and the listing for the property says three of the small second-story rooms are boarded up.

"Are you ready to walk through now or do you want to look at something else?" I ask Anastasia.

"I want to go in. This place intrigues me."

Holding hands, we climb the front porch steps and enter the house through the heavy dark door.

Layers of paint cover the woodwork, and creaks cry out from the floor with each step we take. The smell of dead rodents and mustiness cause us to cover our noses until I pry several of the stuck dining room windows open. Overgrown boxwoods and climbing vines have crept up and attached themselves to the peeling paint and window frames. Apparently, an elderly couple lived in the house for twenty years but did no upkeep. Before them, the place sat empty for years. It's to sell as is, for cash, as no bank will finance it. Anastasia and I spend hours going from room to room.

"It's perfect for us," Anastasia says. "It needs work, but it's on the National Register of Historic Places. Imagine how it must have functioned as a receiving hospital because of the Virginia

Central Railroad Depot being so close."

"Don't you think we should look some more?" I say. "This house will require too much time, work, and money, and we have to make a living. Plus, it will deplete all our savings."

"Nonsense," she says. "It's historic, the price is right, and you know how to do the work. Besides, when my sales take off, you'll be able to quit your job. Then we'll be a team and not dependent on anyone."

"A sane person wouldn't look twice at this house," I say with a sense of doom.

But my wife has that gleam in her eye, and I know I can do the repairs. My adoptive father taught me and, because I was his least favorite son, worked me hard. Spare the rod and spoil the child, he used to say. Especially the adopted child, apparently.

* * *

Anastasia and I will live our married life on Oak Street, with railroad tracks a hundred yards away. I like that we'll be able to sit on the large front porch and drink sweet tea. When the nights turn cool, we can snuggle before one of the two working fireplaces. Plus, there are sidewalks, and when dusk comes, circles of light will shine upon us from the streetlamps. The shadows of the dense trees and bushes behind the house spook me, though I don't understand why.

At closing on October 13, 1949, we are given two skeleton keys, the originals to the house. Two months later, our first child is born.

CHAPTER FOUR

Anastasia

My first child makes his grand entrance after we buy this house, as if he wanted to be born here and no place else. It is all meant to be. The sun rises and sets upon my boy, and my husband and I are filled with glee over our precious prodigy. *Such a beautiful baby and a miracle*, I think as my Golden Prince suckles my breasts.

Five years pass, and a second son, unplanned, enters the world. Clearly, he is not as special as the first. He demands too much attention and batters me down. I find myself trembling, and my swollen bosom dries up.

Three years later, in 1957, a baby girl catches me off guard. When she is placed in my arms, she cries, and I cannot console her as she prefers her father. I do not breastfeed her, but immediately introduce the bottle.

This tiny bundle is not as beautiful as I. She has a sour smell and somber face—an ugly duckling who I hope develops into a swan, but I have my doubts. Perhaps I should smile at her and my second son too, but it is a passing thought and soon forgotten.

I start a baby book for my daughter, but the entries are scarce, not like Golden Prince's, which is filled with daily anecdotes and gold stars.

I never get around to starting a book for Second Son.

* * *

I sit on a stool at the dining room table, which I prefer over a chair because I like to sit up high, as if I am upon a throne. The children are napping, and as I survey my many mounds of paperwork, a satisfied smile crosses my lips. It's 1958, and real estate sales are very good. Today I celebrate. I've received my broker license, a feat practically unheard of for a woman. But since the war, people have been in a hurry to buy their own homes, and I make sure it happens.

I made a wise decision in marrying Bastard Boy. One night in the early stages of our courtship, he drank too much champagne, for that is about all I drink, and told me his tale of sorrow. I listened intently while stroking his face, making him promise never to refer to himself as Bastard Boy again. I realized then that we were a match made in heaven because he, a highly educated handyman, would always be at my beck and call.

Lifting my glass, I sip André Champagne while popping one of my endless supply of Valium. I like how the combination works, making me dreamy and happy. I am Anastasia Romanov's descendant, so I insist on being called by her name. My long-deceased father alluded to it years ago. With my superior intellect—graduating from the university at sixteen—and my taste for finer things, how could it not be true? Plus, I have the same foot deformity as she. I keep all news and magazine articles about the grand duchess's family in a scrapbook.

I don't mind that my husband and I cannot sit at the dining room table to eat. Instead, we take our meals in the living room, using television trays and silver plates. The large table for eight makes a wonderful desk, so I've claimed the entire room as my office.

I find it easy to take money from the poor and make myself rich through real estate trickery. I have done so with no regrets. I finance houses to those who can't afford them, then take them back when the residents can no longer pay my graduating interest rates. I count my coins at the table, having little pity for the serfs fool enough to skip over the fine print, all while my handyman husband looks on.

CHAPTER FIVE

Anastasia

When the trains go by, the house shakes and the windowpanes rattle. It's deemed historic, having stood through the Civil War as a military hospital that served the Glorious South, plus it gives me tax write-offs. I'm convinced I've made an excellent investment. The year 1960 has been a good one for me.

Granted, the house is badly in need of paint and repairs, but I'm too busy building my empire to pay much attention. Besides, that's my husband's department. I'm the breadwinner and can't spend my time on mundane matters.

My daughter, though, worries me. At age three, she marches, stands, and salutes as if part of an army, but no one else is there. I tell her many times that little girls should not play soldier. I don't hear the floorboards creak with the invisible feet of

16

wounded soldiers, but she tells me about the sounds and the injured men who make them. She makes up stories, and if it doesn't stop, I will punish her.

I tell her to imagine she's with Jesus. She's heard stories about him in her Sunday School class, although we don't get there as often as I'd like. She shakes her head no, though, saying Jesus does not come to her even when she offers up her little-girl prayers.

Golden Prince is barely ten when he coughs up blood. The doctors diagnose leukemia, and I pray for a miracle while holding my hands over him like faith healers do. When the doctors retest him, the disease has vanished. So now I know that I have a "sixth sense," particularly with real estate investments.

Once Golden Prince is on his feet again, I decide to rent rooms to common men who can afford no better. My husband creates two additional bedrooms upstairs from boarded chambers that hold discarded boxes and junk.

After a good sweeping, a fresh coat of paint, and the setting of the necessary rat traps, I place advertisements in the paper. Golden Prince doesn't want to share a room with his pesty six-year-old brother, so I put Second Son's bed in the hall, which gives me another room to rent.

It isn't long before male boarders come and go, passing Second Son's cot. Golden Prince and Dutiful Daughter have rooms of their own, with doors that close and lock.

CHAPTER SIX

Anastasia

It is a typical Sunday within the palace walls. In the heat of the July afternoon, Golden Prince practices the piano while a dining room window fan blows in warm air. The scent of honeysuckle pours through the open windows.

Second Son sits on the piano bench turning the pages to "Moonlight Sonata" for his brother. Golden Prince has been taking piano lessons for four years and, at age eleven, surpasses his teachers. Dutiful Daughter, age four, plays quietly with Wolfdog, her imaginary pet. She's a shy child, not at all like her brothers.

We do not go to the park, swim at the local pool, or cook out like other families. We have no real pets, swing sets, sandboxes, bikes, or roller skates like the children down the street do. We don't need such trappings; we have each other.

Stretched out in his faded blue La-Z-Boy recliner, my husband rereads his favorite issue of *Modern Man*, featuring "The Three Lives of Brigitte Bardot—with Six Pages of Sensational Photos!"

I stand by the dining room table holding a spreadsheet of losses to be written off on our taxes while he holds up the spreadsheet of the pornographic Miss Bardot.

I survey the room and smile. "Oh, dear husband, how lovely Miss Bardot is. She's giving me ideas. Let's go to our room and play our favorite records. I'm in the mood for Brenda Lee's 'I Want to Be Wanted.'" I wink at my children and take my husband by the hand. "Boys, watch over your sister. We'll be back soon."

Golden Prince nods in agreement as he fingers the black piano keys. A child prodigy, I'm sure.

Second Son, almost always smelling of peanut butter and jelly, is a curious boy of seven, and a bit neglected, I admit. He gives us time to settle in before pattering down the hall toward our room.

Standing on the other side of our closed bedroom door, Second Son peeks through the keyhole. I'm not surprised. I've caught him at it before.

CHAPTER SEVEN

Second Son

That night, like many others, I count the crusty spots on my sheets. It's what I do in the middle of the blue-black darkness when the texture of the moonlight plays upon the hall ceiling. The male boarders come and go, leaving me small gifts: chewing gum, toy soldiers, and goodnight kisses. I am seven years old.

The house creaks and shifts when the boarders visit me on the way to their rooms. The painful but familiar ache causes me to whimper while they are doing it. After they leave, the dust mites float in the air, and I trace them in the dark.

Before long, I hear snoring coming from their rooms.

* * *

22

Weeks pass by and now I cower in the cellar. I've just thrown rocks and shattered the windshield of a parked car. A man comes out of his house and chases me down the street, but I run fast. I don't think he knows it's me. I will hide here until I know it's safe to come out.

This same man once boarded in our house. For months he stopped by my cot on the way to his room. I was glad to see him leave. Then he purchased a house from Mother and moved up the street. He calls out when he sees me walk by and invites me in. I hate him... I hate him... I hate him!

CHAPTER EIGHT

Bastard Man

"Father, there's a lady at the door for you," four-year-old Cinderella says as she enters my bedroom.

I look at the bedroom clock. Its 9:00 a.m. and Sunday. "Did she say who she is or what she wants?"

"No, but she says it's important."

I get up and put my bathrobe on over my pajamas. It's probably a tenant angry about a burst water pipe or a leaky toilet. Anastasia is still asleep, snoring lightly, probably having taken a sleeping pill before bed. She seldom gets up before ten except for the Sundays she wants us to go to church.

"May I help you?" I ask the middle-aged woman at the door.

She's holding an umbrella, and it's a cold, wet day in November 1961. "It's you!" she says. "I know it is! It's me, Adrian, your sister. I've been on a search for you for months, and today's the day! May I come in?"

"It's not a good idea," I say, shocked at her unannounced visit. "The family's sleeping. Why didn't you call instead of just showing up? If you could locate my address, you easily could have found the number."

"I wanted to see your face when you saw me after such a long time. I thought you'd be excited to connect with your family." She cocked her head. "You are glad to see me, aren't you? We've so much to talk about."

"I'd like you to go back to your car and wait for me. This needs to be a private conversation."

I close the door, go back upstairs, and change out of my pajamas. My hands shake, and when I look in the bathroom mirror, I see I've turned a ghastly white. I slowly go downstairs, knowing nothing good will come of this encounter.

Luckily, Cinderella is the only one up, and she's busy watching cartoons in the living room. Sheet music, dirty clothes, and books are scattered all around her. "I'm going outside for a while, baby girl," I say as I grab my overcoat from the overflowing tree rack by the front door. "I shouldn't be long."

I get into the passenger side of a new green Buick. It looks like Adrian has done all right for herself. "How did you find me?" I say, hearing the irritated edge to my voice.

"Our mother died all alone last year. Phil found her on the kitchen floor after she didn't answer the phone for several days. She lived a hard life, you know."

I could tell Adrian wanted me to say something, but I let her keep talking as I stared out the windshield.

"She did the best she could," Adrian said as if pleading her case to a judge. "I mean, we all knew she drank, but none of us could get her to stop. That's what she died from, you know."

"The drink?"

"Yes. Alcohol poisoning Probably did it to deal with her never-ending depression. But still, it was a shock to all of us. You know, she did the best she could raising us, mainly cleaning other people's houses."

"I don't know what you want me to say. I was too young to remember much of that."

"Well, it might interest you to know that when I cleaned out her room, I found a notebook underneath her slips and bras. It contained the names of the men who took you, along with a baby picture. I located and talked to each of them. At first, no one would tell me anything, then the pharmacist broke his silence and told me who adopted you."

"And this is supposed to mean something to me?"

"Well, yes. She never got over losing you. She still had that one baby picture. That has to mean something."

"Go on," I said, not really wanting to hear any more.

"From there it wasn't hard. Your adopted father still lives at the same address, and he told me where you went to college. He says he hasn't heard from you in years."

"My other siblings—do they know you've found me?"

"I didn't want to say anything until I was sure. I don't work, and I'm the only one who had the time and money to locate you. I want it to be a big surprise for the family!"

"What makes you think I want to be found?" My anger rises. "Can you possibly comprehend what it's been like for me? When I look in my children's faces, I see my brothers and sisters and remember the night my mother gave me away like the unwanted runt of the litter. How can I ever be a good father after what was done to me?"

"But I thought you'd—"

"Do you think everything turned out fine because I got adopted and graduated from college? You have no idea what it was like to be acquired by a rich man who was supposed to act like a father but didn't. You have no idea what I endured. And now you show up here, a do-gooder and busybody, and want to interrupt my life and make everything okay for you? You need to drive away from here and never come back." I get out of the car and slam the door on her stunned face.

She unrolls her window and calls out to me. "Please! Come back and let's discuss this further. If not today, another day?"

"I'll never talk to you or any of my siblings. I have my wife and that's enough. Now leave and never return."

When I go back into the house, Cinderella is waiting for me.

"Are you all right, Father? You look funny."

I get down on my knees, wanting to hug her, but I can't. Adrian's four-year-old face is looking back at me.

CHAPTER NINE

Bastard Man

Although Anastasia and I are both thirty-nine, I look much older. Sun damage and the toll of cigarettes line my ruddy face. My wife, an avid user of moisturizers and creams, never leaves the house without being perfumed and powdered. To me, she's still a real beauty, even after thirteen years of marriage and three children.

Anastasia likes to play Lady of the House and Repairman while at our vacant properties. She enters first. I wait a few minutes, then knock.

"Who is it?" she says with a provocative voice.

"You called for a repairman," I answer. Then she opens the door. Sometimes she's wearing a sexy nighty she's stashed in her purse; often she wears nothing but a string of pearls. Anastasia never tires of the game, and I'm always willing to spice things up.

If my wife is in a mischievous mood, she lets us into a house that's on the market. She gets really excited imagining how a real estate agent could walk in on us with clients. She particularly likes open houses.

Whenever I accompany Anastasia, I wear my tool belt about my waist. There is no telling what my beloved wife might ask me to fix or do. If something tickles her fancy, I'm ready. I always carry lubricant, which can be used for many things.

CHAPTER TEN

Dutiful Daughter

I beg Mother for a night-light, but she says no because I'm in the first grade and too old for one. I don't tell her that Golden Prince opens my bedroom door and watches me. He warns me not to tell my parents and that if I do, I'll be punished for lying.

"Please protect me from my brother," I say to Sunday School Jesus as I huddle under my covers and fight the draft from the January cold. "I don't want to play tickle monster again." But once again, Jesus does not answer my prayer, so I pray to Wolfdog instead.

Golden Prince plays the piano for hours. I hate it when he plays, because it means he's in the living room and might come for me. Yet I'm nervous when he doesn't play, because then I don't know where he is.

Golden Prince's piano-playing fingers move all over me. I push him away with my little-girl hands, but it does not stop him. I'm only six.

He finds me hiding in my closet, the basement, and the bathroom. I know what is going to happen; his wicked eyes tell me. There is no point in struggling. Witnessing the fear in my face, he smiles.

When my parents leave the house to show real estate, Golden Prince babysits me. He always wants to play naughty games, which more times than not require him to give me a bath. "You're dirty down there," he says. "I need to wash between your legs."

When he is finished with me, I stand naked in front of the bathroom mirror and see my heart crying. I should wash my face and brush my hair, I tell the mirror. No use, the mirror replies.

* * *

I can't pay attention in school, and my teacher scolds me. We've been practicing naming the months of the year and days of the week, but I don't get it right. "Today is January 22,

1963," she tells me, pointing at the chalkboard with her ruler.

When I look out the classroom window, I see Wolfdog standing in a light dusting of snow. He comes often now, especially when I am screaming in my dreams. Wolfdog lets me know Golden Prince's thoughts and tells me when he's coming, often giving me time to get away. He's found a new hiding place for me— in the bushes behind the house. I wish he would bare his teeth and kill my brother.

CHAPTER ELEVEN

Anastasia

The Feminine Mystique by Betty Friedan comes out in April 1963. I read about it in the *New York Times* and get my copy as soon as I can, devouring it immediately. Friedan understands me in a way no one else does. I had no idea that so many women shared my strange stirrings and sense of dissatisfaction. I never should have become a mother. No, that's not true, but we should have stopped with Golden Prince. Twice the condom broke. Unbelievable!

I'm not one for making beds, washing clothes, or preparing anything besides sandwiches, much less doing toilet training or chauffeuring little beasts. I'll never give up my dreams or get caught in a domestic squirrel cage. No, not me!

I visit our family physician and get another prescription for Valium. Not that I need it now, but I like how it makes me feel, so I play my doctor's game to get the refills. Depression is my official diagnosis—what a laugh. Mother's Little Helper is more like it.

I think back to the day I snooped through my childhood attic and discovered a journal tucked away behind an old credenza. I opened it to the first faded page and was shocked by the contents. Mother was married before Father! Apparently, I wasn't an only child. Somewhere I had a half-sister. Mother's first husband beat her and had alcoholic rages, so she left in the middle of the night with their infant. Then she met Father, a widowed Methodist minister thirty years her senior. He helped her place the child for adoption but also took a liking to Mother's looks and desperation, so he took her in. After Mother's divorce was final, she agreed to marry Father, but only if she could have another child. That was where the journal ended.

Two years later, I arrived in the family. Father doted on me and called me Princess. When I got big enough, he read me stories and had me memorize Bible verses, rewarding me with sweet treats as I sat on his fat belly in his large brown swivel chair. As far back as I can remember, Father hurled insults at Mother. She didn't press his shirts smoothly enough or act as perfectly as his dead spouse had, but I grew accustomed to hearing his complaints. I used to hate how Mother wore only dowdy housedresses and would never stand up to him, always crying and whimpering instead. She was so weak. I will never be like her. Never!

I was proud of Father, though. Churchgoers hung on his every word. Father picked out and bought me beautiful clothes, and I held his hand as the congregation members filed out of church. Mother would clutch her purse tightly and say nothing, often waiting in the car. From her sad face, I could tell she hated being his wife, and I used to wonder if she was thinking about the baby she gave away.

Once I started first grade, Mother took a job as an assistant kindergarten teacher. Father liked the idea of her making money and contributing to the family's finances. Plus, he wasn't getting any younger and wanted to slow down.

At night, though, I could hear Mother crying in her bedroom. I used to find bottles of peach brandy under the kitchen sink and behind the sheets in the linen closet. My parents never shared a bed that I can remember—yet another reason to believe I'm adopted. Good God, I bet Mother never had an orgasm in her life!

But both my parents are dead now. There's no use in crying over spilled milk.

Betty Friedan concludes her first chapter with: "We can no longer ignore that voice within women that says: 'I want something more than my husband and my children and my house.'"

I wish Mother could have read this book, but I doubt she could have comprehended its message. I have my career. No one can make me a prisoner of suburbia and they'd better not try. The book changes my life. Such a pioneering philosophy! But it's time to get going. I need a dose of nicotine, a Valium, and a shot of liquor. Hair of the dog that bit me after last night's real estate party.

CHAPTER TWELVE

Second Son

Most Sundays my family sits in the second pew at the Methodist church on Broad Street. My grandfather on my mother's side was a Methodist minister with a nice singing voice, but he died before I was born. I'm told I sang with the hymnal upside down when I was too young to read.

Choirmaster hears my voice and invites me to sing in the Episcopal Boys Choir. This is an honor, and Mother brags to the congregation about me, something she's never done before.

Choirmaster offers words of encouragement and invites me for special and very private lessons at his home. My first lesson is on May 1, 1964. I think it's important to remember this.

* * *

At ten years old, I can walk to Choirmaster's house as it is just down the street. Most of the houses look alike with big porches, sidewalks in front, and trees dotting the yards. Choirmaster says I have a beautiful tenor voice, and I am proud I can do something better than Golden Prince.

There is a plate of chocolate chip cookies and a glass of milk waiting for me in the dingy, unfinished basement. After several toasts of sherry to loosen up my voice, Choirmaster and I eat cookies, play Old Maid, Go Fish, and then "Little Jack Horner." I don't like it when Choirmaster caresses my bum, sticks in his thumb, and, with a shuddering moan, tells me what a good boy I am.

When the games finish, the singing begins. I want to stop the lessons, but Mother insists I continue. I do not want to disappoint her.

It isn't long before I open my mouth and spew out bony dry sounds with no flavor or pitch, only the faint trickle of hollow notes.

CHAPTER THIRTEEN

Dutiful Daughter

Father believes in hard work. He's up and out of the house early with a list of things Mother wants done to her properties. But first he opens the box of Raisin Bran and counts the raisins in his bowl. He has to have twenty-three; I don't know why. Sometimes he has to pick more raisins out of the box or put some back in.

Today, he fishes out one more raisin. Then he adds milk and lots of sugar, eats in a hurry, and leaves.

I pick his dishes up from the table and take them to the sink. The trash hasn't been taken out for days, maybe weeks, and it's piling up. The greasy pots and pans on the stove need to be scrubbed. Even when I try, I can't get them clean. I wonder if other people keep all their old newspapers and magazines around. At our house, there are piles of them everywhere.

You can set your watch that Father will be home for his TV dinner and to watch Walter Cronkite on the six-thirty news, or at least that's what Mother says. It's my job to set up the TV trays in the living room so we can all watch the program together.

On the rare days Father finishes work early, he sits on the front porch, drinks a beer containing three raw eggs, and throws darts at circles he's painted on a board that hangs on a house column.

My father catches mice in the house, using traps and poison.

"Please let me keep two or three," I plead one late afternoon. "I'd like to have a pet, and they're so cute. I'll keep them in a cage and take good care of them, I promise."

"They leave droppings and bring disease and multiply like mice do," he says with a chuckle. "Plus, your mother would never go for it."

There is no use in arguing, and I don't want to know what Father does when he catches the mice, so I go in the house and set up the TV trays as usual. As I do, I apologize to the mice. "I wanted to give you a safe home, and I would have been a good mother.

I'm truly sorry."

By 6:20 p.m., we are all seated with our food. I'm having the Swanson Salisbury steak—it's my favorite—while my parents eat turkey dinners. I don't pay attention to what my brothers are eating, but it's probably fried chicken.

After watching Walter Cronkite, *The Ed Sullivan Show* comes on. Mr. Sullivan says, "Ladies and gentlemen, the Beatles!" The fab four play three songs—"All My Loving," "Till There Was You," and "She Loves You."

I don't know what to think when the girls in the audience go crazy, but I know I like Simon and Garfunkel more than I like this group. My parents watch and laugh as my brothers dance around the room like they're part of the band.

Just before going on break, Mr. Sullivan comes back on stage and says, "This day, February 9, 1964, will go down in history for a group called the Beatles."

CHAPTER FOURTEEN

Second Son

I am in the basement waiting for my voice lesson to begin. Choirmaster has left me alone. Waiting, waiting, waiting, I hear men laughing in another room.

Choirmaster comes in and tells me to close my eyes. I do, and Choirmaster puts something in my mouth. I swallow. "That's good," Choirmaster says. "That is very, very good." The other men come in, one by one, waiting for their turn to feed me.

* * *

Morning light falls on the blooming summer roses as I look out the living room window. I wonder if the flowers fear the autumn season fast approaching. My birthday is in the fall. It's 1965, I will be eleven, and I have begun to stutter.

I am still gazing out as Old Man Tate, rigid with pursed lips and beady eyes, walks his dog. It won't be long before he calls me on the phone wanting his snow shoveled. He tells other men in the neighborhood about me. The men call me by my new name, Pissant, and I hate it. Yet I never say no to the ten dollars and forbidden activity. I do not think I am allowed to. Still, I should tell someone about Old Man Tate, Choirmaster, and the others. Maybe write a note to a teacher or a police officer.

I wonder about telling Golden Prince, but Choirmaster tells me my brother already knows. He says that Golden Prince sometimes watches through the window, and haven't I noticed when the purple drapes have been left open? I've never seen him there and don't believe it, but now I pay attention to the window and the purple drapes that look like hanging choir robes.

"If you tell what we do here, my friends and I will hurt your family," Choirmaster has said. "A fire in the night? You wouldn't want that on your conscience, would you? Or perhaps your little sister goes missing."

I squeeze my pencil so tightly that I break the lead. Another pencil, a looser grip. No matter, I have nothing to say. I've forgotten how to breathe, and I cry without tears.

CHAPTER FIFTEEN

Bastard Man

In public, I make no insignificant gestures. Having a great sense of humor and style, with my dyed red hair and leisure suits, I love to be the center of attention and should be. I own an Arabian, after all. Anastasia and I acquired the horse from a tenant with huge gambling debts. Instead of evicting him for nonpayment of rent, we worked out a deal. Lady Day's been with us for ten years now, and the tenant's been gone for nine.

How I relish these few moments that make me feel like a successful man in my own right, when Anastasia isn't around to steal my thunder. I think of excuses to leave the house before she awakens from her afternoon naps: a trip to the bank, the purchase of a tool, whatever I can think of.

Pissant and Cinderella

When my daughter accompanies me, I tell everyone her name is Cinderella, knowing they won't forget it. I have her memorize and tell dirty jokes in order to horrify strangers and get a laugh. At eight, she's too young to understand what she's saying, and before long she answers to her new name.

In elevators, stairwells, and bank lobbies, I jovially pull out pictures of my Arabian. I have no pictures of my children to show. Plus, everyone has children, but I am a man with an Arabian, which I plan to breed as often as I can. That surely counts for something. It's 1965, and by the end of 1967, I hope to own two more of the impressive beasts.

But I have worries. Our palace is slowly decaying. Cracks mar the mortar, the chimneys are crumbling, and the weeds pile up against the driveway and front steps. Anastasia seems not to notice the rot, but it keeps me busy from morning to night as I try to stay ahead of the building inspectors. Golden Prince, at fifteen, is old enough to help me, but Anastasia won't allow it.

"He's too good for that," she says. "What if he hurts his delicate piano-playing fingers?"

For the first time in my married life, I have the urge to slap her.

The weather grows hot and sticky, creeping into the mid-nineties as I scrape and sand the peeling paint from the woodwork of the 1920s shotgun house. Exhausted and sweaty, my muscles cramping, I paint the kitchen, living room, and bathroom, and then haul out boxes of trash. All to prepare for the next renter. My wife evicts tenants after they're late with their rent or mortgage payments a third time. She wants this work finished tomorrow so she can rent out the property over the Fourth of July weekend. I need to hurry. Anastasia always knows someone who can pay more.

That night I thrash around in bed, unable to get comfortable because of overworked muscles and a persistent cough. Anastasia sends me to the living room couch.

"You don't mind, do you, darling? I need my beauty sleep."

While I lie there, I greet two late-night boarders as they return from their three-to-eleven shifts at the steel plant. We chat briefly before they climb the stairs, passing Second Son's cot on the way to their rooms. Nice enough fellows, and they always pay their rent on time.

CHAPTER SIXTEEN

Cinderella

I'm at the kitchen table eating a bowl of Frosted Flakes when Mother comes into the kitchen and picks up the newspaper.

"I can't believe it's 1966, and April to boot. This year is flying by, Cinderella."

"Why can't you believe it, Mother?"

"Real estate is selling fast, not that I'm complaining, but I'm too busy to go to the grocery store today. I've got a house showing, and since it's Saturday, I want you to pull your wagon to Ferrell's Market and get what we need. There's no reason you can't do it since you're a big girl of nine."

The old rickety wagon, wooden with high sides, could do with a thick coat of paint. I wouldn't be so embarrassed if it were a red Radio Flyer, but Mother laughs when I ask for one. "Things cost money, dear. One day you'll understand that."

"What do you want me to get at Ferrell's?" I ask.

"I'll make out a list. Would you get me a pen and a piece of paper? That's a good girl. And an envelope too. I'm glad your father made coffee before he left this morning."

I wash my bowl and put it away as she sips her coffee. It's almost 10:00 a.m., and I'm the only one in the house except for her. I put the items she asks for on the table.

"I want you to get three—no, make that five—of the Swanson turkey dinners. Your father is partial to their cornbread dressing and sweet potatoes. Pick up four of the fried chicken and five of the Salisbury steak. Make sure you get the four-compartment trays with the apple cobbler and brownies. If they have a good deal on navel oranges, pick up a bag. Also, some milk, three cans of pintos, hot dogs, and buns."

"That's a lot to get," I say as Mother pulls a silver mirror from her purse and pencils in her eyebrows.

"You can do it. I've got a busy week ahead, and so does your father. Actually, there are a few more things I need to add: eggs, a head of cabbage, a red onion, and a box each of Grape Nuts and Wheaties." Mother sets her eyebrow pencil down and writes out the rest of her list.

"I hope all of this will fit in the wagon," I say, worried about pulling home such a big load.

"Mr. Ferrell will help you. I'm giving you cash and a little extra to put on our account. Make sure you don't lose it." Mother rummages through her purse, pulls out money, and puts it into the envelope. After taking a deep drink of coffee, she gets up from the table and leaves.

I get dressed and go looking for the wagon. It's in the back of the house and full of Father's tools, which I unload and put on the porch. At least it's a nice day to walk the five blocks to Ferrell's Market.

* * *

"Well, young lady, what have you got there?" says Mr. Ferrell when I enter his store. He's a friendly man with a big grin and a perfect comb-over for his bald head.

"Mother's list and the money to pay for it," I say, feeling nervous, though I shouldn't be.

"I'll get everything together. Pick out something from the candy jar while you wait. It won't take but a few minutes. We've been a little slow today."

Before I know it, I'm loaded up and walking home sucking on a red Tootsie Roll Pop. I've gone only two blocks when I see my brother rushing down the front steps of Choirmaster's house.

"Never come this way again!" he yells as he approaches me. "Go around the block next time. Promise."

"Okay." He's so upset, I think it best not to ask him why. "Do you want to walk home with me now?"

"Sure, let's go."

We walk for a few minutes before I speak again. "Do you like being the second son?"

"No, I hate it."

"I hate being a girl."

He reaches over and puts his hand on the wagon handle, covering mine. We pull it home together.

CHAPTER SEVENTEEN

Pissant

I like the beauty and loneliness of winter, the sound of ice cracking in the trees, chattering teeth, short days, and long nights, unless the boarders stop by my bed. I'm now twelve and my stuttering has grown worse, although it doesn't happen when I sing.

Father says that the winter of 1966 will be one of the coldest in years. Donning a jacket and gloves, I step outside and stop to watch cars creeping down the road, pushing deep tracks through the snow.

A dark Plymouth pulls to the side of the road, across from our house, and the driver emerges. He is older, with craggy skin drooping from his face like a dirty bedsheet, and he has only a fringe of black hair on the sides of his large round head. His movements are deliberate, his eyes sharp and watchful. He looks my way.

It's been a year since I've seen him. His calloused hands pawed at me in Choirmaster's bedroom. I struggled, then froze when his arms pinned me down. His hand groped downward, plunging into my pants. When he tried to force his thing in me, he failed. In that split second, I struck him in the crotch, then I grabbed his stack of Polaroid pictures by the bed, fled through Choirmaster's bedroom door, and dashed outside.

I hid in the bushes, camouflaged by pouring rain and wet leaves as he looked for me. He got so close that I saw his dirty black fingernails and smelled his rancid odor. He reeked of splattered fat from cooked bacon.

I got away then, but now he's back.

I watch as he puts on sunglasses, and I remember how scared I was of the deep lines etched between his eyebrows. I pull my baseball cap down low on my face and hope he won't notice me. Too late.

His words call me to attention, like a dog hearing its master's commands, but I ignore him and walk the opposite way. When

I return two hours later, his car is gone, but I remain afraid because now he knows where I live.

I draw the blinds down tight in the living room so he can't look in. Freezing rain pelts the windows, reminding me of the man's ice-cold hands. Lying on the living room couch, I stare at the shadows on the ceiling created by the streetlights that filter through the blinds.

Shutting my eyes, I try to sleep, but when I do, I feel like I'm falling, and my breathing becomes fast and shallow. I rise from the couch, go to the kitchen, pour a glass of milk, and drink it. That night I dream of the man's watery blue eyes and womanly breasts.

The next morning, I pull out the stolen Polaroid pictures that I hid beneath a box of Father's old work boots in the attic. There are six, and I'm not in any of them, but others are. I know three of the boys, all much younger than me. This is wrong, very wrong, and I want to help. In two of the pictures, the man is doing things to five-year-old Tommy in the dark Plymouth. I know it's the same man because of the dirty fingernails.

I slip out of the house, keeping the horrible images in my pocket. I know where Tommy lives. I pick up a discarded dog collar from a neighbor's yard. If anyone asks me what I'm doing, I'm looking for my lost pet.

At Tommy's house, I quietly climb onto the porch and peek through a living room window. No neighbors are outside, so I'm in the clear. Most of the family is in the kitchen eating breakfast, but Tommy is watching cartoons on the couch while shoveling down cereal.

I stroll to the driveway as if looking for my dog, and I find the family car unlocked. I open it, place the pictures faceup on the driver's seat, and rush home.

Two days later, on the front page of the paper, an article tells of an unexplained car explosion behind a deserted warehouse. A dark Plymouth was consumed in flames, the victim too badly burned to be identified. Tommy's father is a cop.

CHAPTER EIGHTEEN

Cinderella

"This morning we're going to the stables," Mother tells me as she pours her coffee. "I want you to meet our new filly, Chestnut. She arrived yesterday, so put on your riding clothes."

"Do I have to?" I say. "No one else wears an English riding habit."

"If Elizabeth Taylor can wear one in National Velvet, you can too. I'd think you'd be grateful. Most girls would be. When you come back, I want to see you in your jodhpurs, chaps, and riding boots. And bring your jacket. It's April, but it might not warm up much today."

"How come my brothers don't have to do this?"

56

"Lessons cost money, so I'll only pay for one of my children to ride. I think the experience would be good for you, and you're my only daughter, after all. If you learn to ride well, you can be in competitions and maybe meet the right caliber of people. Even though you're only ten, connections matter."

While we're in the car, Father won't stop talking about Arabian horses. "The Bedouins trace Arabians back to 3000 B.C. They kept meticulous records and used the horses for transportation, hauling loads, and war mounts. Did you know that Genghis Khan, Napoleon Bonaparte, George Washington, and Alexander the Great owned and rode Arabians? It may be 1967, but historically, we're in splendid company."

"Why don't you and Mother ride?" I say when he finally stops for a breath.

"We'd rather admire the Arabians, make money, and keep them as a hobby. But I sure like the horse shows, and so does your mother. We meet interesting people, some of which your mother can sell real estate to."

"In my business," Mother says, "it helps to know the right people. You'll recognize that as you get older, Cinderella."

"I'm trying to talk your mother into getting a stud," Father says with a laugh. "I'd like to have one."

"I've read up on it," Mother says. "Stallions are full of testosterone and are a lot of trouble. Maybe if it goes well with the fillies, we can get one later. But I've been told they can overwhelm the pocketbook, and I don't like that."

Thirty minutes later, we're at the stables. Luke, the owner, comes out to meet us as we pile out of the station wagon. He's wearing jeans, cowboy boots, and a denim shirt with a bandanna around his neck. I can't help but notice how much he looks like Adam on *Bonanza*, my favorite television show.

"You've got a beauty with two-year-old Chestnut," he says to Mother. "They brought her to us last evenin'. She's in her stall if you want to take a look."

"How long will it be before I can breed her?" Mother says, not even glancing toward the barn that holds her new filly.

"They should be four before they're bred," Luke says.

"Ridiculous," Mother says. "That's much too long to wait."

"Bein' in foal and growin' at the same time puts additional stress on the horse. Are you plannin' to ride and break Chestnut to saddle?"

58

"Yes, that's my plan."

"If you go against my recommendation to wait, you shouldn't do anything except give Chestnut light exercise and plenty of pasture time. Mares are the most fertile in the spring and early summer, and gestation is eleven months. Keep in mind that the summer heat can be an extreme stress, and the risks are greater."

"I hear what you're saying, Luke, but I don't agree," Mother says. "I plan on doing it my way. And there's something else. I'd like to increase my daughter's riding lessons with you to twice a month."

"That can be arranged," Luke says. "I'm free on Saturday mornings round about ten."

"Fine. Now please get Lady Day ready for Cinderella to mount. I want to take pictures I can use later." She dismisses Luke, who returns to the stable.

A minute later Luke leads Lady Day out and helps me climb on her back, but I almost fall while mounting. It doesn't help that my parents watch.

"Remember your posture, Cinderella," Mother says while telling me how to pose for the photos. I hate having my picture taken because it gives Mother another version of me to criticize.

I'd rather be in the stall playing with the new filly.

Mother keeps her agreement with Luke and takes me to the stables two Saturdays a month. I hate the thirty-minute drive with her as she makes endless comments on how I can improve myself. By the time we get to the stables, I'm a nervous wreck and can't wait to get out of the car. But at least it's always a relief to see Luke. As usual, he tips his cowboy hat at me and says, "Howdy, ma'am." He doesn't do that for Mother.

"If I'm gonna teach your girl to ride well," Luke says to Mother, "I'm gonna have to ask you to leave and come back in a couple hours."

"Make it an hour and I'll wait in the car," Mother says.

"When young'uns become a certain age, I don't allow parents to watch the lessons. It slows their progress. Sorry, ma'am, but those are my terms."

Mother huffs away, murmuring under her breath, then gets in her station wagon and speeds off. My admiration for Luke grows in that moment because no one talks to Mother like that. I'm beyond tickled that I'll get to ride and be with him twice a month.

Linda Kay Simmons

"Now that you've had several lessons with me," Luke says, "let's review what you've learned so far. Lesson One: Fear is fear, and it don't matter if you got two legs or four. Horses are sensitive creatures. They know what you're feelin', so always show 'em kindness.

"Lesson Two: Horses can be scary because of their size and apparent skittishness, so it's natural you want to protect yourself. But Chestnut is as solid and gentle as they come, so don't worry 'bout being bucked off. It's more about you bein' fearful than the horse, especially with you bein' a fairly new rider and all. Got that?"

I nod. My first riding lessons were nothing like this. A middle-aged woman had led me around by the reins while I sat on Lady Day. But Luke is a genuine cowboy, the kind you see in Westerns. I bet he's in his late twenties, but I'll never have the nerve to ask. I love his cowboy twang and the way he chews on a piece of straw.

"It's time to mount Chestnut," he says.

With his help, I sit on her back while keeping a death grip on the reins. Chestnut is more rambunctious than Lady Day.

"You know," he says, "I've had a few difficulties in my life, but

61

life has a way of just keepin' on. All I can say is never let fear stop you from gettin' what you want, young lady—or make you do somethin' you don't want. So I need to ask, Do you really want to learn to ride or is this your mother's idea?"

I never thought about it like that. I'm so used to doing whatever Mother says without question. But being with Luke, who's unlike anybody I've ever met, I make an instant decision.

"Yes," I say. "I want to ride. But I don't want to look like Elizabeth Taylor in these fancy clothes."

Luke laughs big, his blue eyes twinkling. "We'll see what we can do about that, then."

The lesson continues, and the time flies by. Chestnut doesn't seem to care how large or small I am, or if I'm wearing the right outfit or not.

When the time is up, we take Chestnut to the stall, and Luke shows me how to brush her down.

"Now give her this sugar cube and thank her for today," he says.

I look into Chestnut's big brown eyes and she into mine. "Thank you, Chestnut, for letting me ride on your back, and for being my friend."

I take the cube from Luke, place it in my outstretched hand, and feed it to Chestnut. "She loves it," I squeal as her big horse lips accept my gift. Happiness runs through me.

"With each lesson, you'll gain ground," Luke says. "Before you know it, you'll be ridin' paths and makin' your own small victories. So, tell me what you learned today."

"Think about knowledge, not about fear," I say.

Luke smiles at me as Mother honks the horn repeatedly.

CHAPTER NINETEEN

Golden Prince

The United States has suffered over eighteen hundred casualties in the Vietnam War. I'll be turning eighteen soon and, without a college deferment, could get drafted if my lottery number is low enough. Luckily, Mother surprises me with her purchase of a 1963 Volkswagen Bus. "This is for you to help me with the business," she says. "Your father's truck is old and undependable. I'll hold onto the title, and the Volkswagen will be in the business's name, but I might let you use it if you collect payments and help with evictions."

"That's great, Mother. I'd be happy to do that for you."

My financial security lies in sucking up to Mother, so I'll collect the damn rents and mortgage payments, and give eviction notices. At least I'll have freedom to come and go with the VW bus; this could end up being a wonderful thing, but my mind is still on being drafted.

Canada, maybe?

No, I have to find another way; the winters are too cold.

President Johnson ended the marriage deferment, so that won't work. If I flee to a neutral country, like Mexico, I'll be a draft dodger, but crossing the border might be my only option. Father will think I'm a coward, but I don't care. I'm not one for following the herd. On the other hand, I'd sure like the feel of an M-16 in my hands.

That night while watching Cronkite from my beanbag chair, I surrender to the growing mellowness of the Mary Jane I'm smoking. I'll figure something out; I always do. Ignorant people have ignorant beliefs, and I'm not one of them. Then the answer comes to me—something Cronkite says about homosexuals and the war. I'll claim to be one of them. I laugh loudly at the idea. I've solved the problem, I gloat inwardly as I take another toke.

CHAPTER TWENTY

Golden Prince

November 22, 1967, is a sunny, cloudless day. After lunch, Mother has me go with her to see her recent purchases. More dumps. A cluster of wood-sided buildings, badly in need of paint and repair, greets me when I get out of her station wagon.

"I got a great deal by buying four," she says. "And at a rock-bottom price."

Poor people with large families and bad-paying jobs always seem to find my mother, or perhaps she finds them. Strange, lonely men with pensions, who are simply waiting to die, are her favorite clientele.

"I never use my own money," she says. "I always take out a second mortgage on my existing properties to buy more." She gives me a wink. "I'm so glad you're in the business with me. Now I can teach you the ropes." She gestures to the dilapidated structures. "Just think, this will all be yours someday."

I pity the poor fools she finances to; it doesn't take long before they fall behind on their loans, not having read the fine print, and find themselves evicted. The property is then returned to Mother to be sold again. Father says nothing; he seldom does. Mother is the brains, and he's the brawn. At least that's what she says.

* * *

The next day Mother invites me to dinner at a fancy restaurant to celebrate my birthday.

"Sorry, Mother, but I don't want to go. I had my draft physical this morning, and I need to tell you what I did."

She listens as I explain my actions and my reasoning. "Let me be the one to tell your father," she says when I'm done. "It will cushion the blow, and he'll get over it with time. We all know it's not true."

"I hope you're right," I say. "But I don't think he'll take it well."

I wonder what Father's reaction would be if he knew I wore

lacy woman's underwear for my physical. I didn't tell Mother that detail.

"If you're sure you don't mind your father and me going to your birthday dinner without you, we will," Mother says. "But I'll bring you back a piece of cake." She puts her hand in her purse, pulls out a small box, and hands it to me. "This was my father's pocket watch, and I want you to have it." She smiles as I examine it.

"Thanks, Mother," I say. "What a great gift!"

Once Mother's gone, I shove the watch in my dresser drawer, knowing I'll never carry it. But who knows? Maybe it'll end up being worth something. Feeling hunger pangs, I go to the kitchen, make myself a turkey sandwich, and pop a cold beer. Settling down on the living room couch, I turn on the TV and eat.

Walter Cronkite comes on at 6:30 p.m., and I don't want to miss his commentaries on Vietnam. Plus, I need to thank him for keeping me safe from the war. I'm a homosexual, according to the draft department. I laugh out loud as I light a joint, then reach for a bowl of M&M's, thinking of myself as a gay deceiver.

CHAPTER TWENTY-ONE

Cinderella

I cook and clean, but it does little good. The palace floors are rotting, and plaster falls from the walls. Bags of string, ropes, wires, cans, and clothes lie everywhere, as well as boxes of newspapers and magazines. My parents claim that all this stuff is too good to throw away and might be useful someday, but it's too much work for anyone to keep up with, much less me, a child of eleven. Not only that but Mother refuses to pay for household repairs or a maid, spending her money on Arabians instead.

As I clean the pantry, I talk to the angels and Wolfdog, my spirit animal. At night I play alone with my Ouija Board. Sometimes a confederate soldier comes through and spells out messages using words I don't understand.

Often during the day, I watch Father walk through the dining room, passing the large rectangular piece of wood in its center while cussing under his breath. He has done this for as long as I can remember. The table is large and awkward and has no seating except for the cushioned stool Mother sits her bulbous behind on while drinking champagne and reviewing her ledgers.

"I want this table out of the house," Father says. "It's been here far too long."

"But it's my desk, darling, don't you see?" Mother says. "No worries for you."

I watch Father's stubbly jaw go tight and his knuckles go white as he attacks it with his carving knife. He does not blink; he never does when he gouges nonsensical words and images of flames and lightning bolts into the hard walnut.

* * *

I try to outsmart Golden Prince, but it's useless. I'm nothing but an ugly, stupid eleven-year-old girl. He pushes me into his room, and when I struggle, it gets worse.

I try to fight him off of the mattress on his floor. But he only laughs and grabs my wrists. The more I wrestle, the more he hurts me. His heart beats against my chest, his breathing heavy. When he's finished with me, he smiles, and the devil dances in his eyes. His hands grasp my hair. "I have a surprise for you," he says. "Pissant is here. You and I are going to help him figure out if he can do it with a girl."

CHAPTER TWENTY-TWO

Pissant

Mother often tells me, Do what Golden Prince tells you; after all, he does no wrong and always makes us proud.

My only brother, nineteen, passed the MENSA exam on October 15, 1968, according to the certificate. He's now a member of the largest and oldest IQ society in the world, and my parents are glowing almost as much as he. "Golden Prince is a genius," Mother coos, her nose pointed skyward. "He inherited his brilliance from me, no doubt. Five thousand alphabetized books in his room, and he's read them all."

My brother snickers at this. He also has Father's cast-off girlie magazines and has shown me the pictures. He tells me the different ways to have sex with females, including my sister.

"Don't worry," he says to me in a confidential fashion, his arm slung around my shoulder. "I've shown the magazines to Cinderella. She won't be surprised by what you do to her. Don't you want to know if you like girls? Tonight, I'm going to give you the chance—or are you only a pissant with old queers?"

"How do you know about that?" I say, shaking with rage and humiliation.

"Everyone knows you take it in the ass and suck cock. Do as I say tonight, and I won't tell Father. It can be our special secret." He clutches me in tighter, pinching my skin. "You want to be a good brother, don't you?"

Golden Prince takes me to Cinderella's room, where I hide in the closet until he's ready for me. I don't have a choice. My mind separates from my body and floats somewhere else while my brain follows my genius brother's instructions.

Fearful of Father finding out my dirty secrets and desperate for my brother's approval, I do what Golden Prince says and feel my familiar shame. My brother's validation does not come.

That night I hear Cinderella sobbing late into the night. My parents lie in ignorance. They sleep with their door closed and a fan on so as not to be disturbed by us, their seemingly unwanted offspring, except for Golden Prince, of course. I want to go to my sister, to comfort her, but I don't dare. I've hurt her the way others have hurt me. She will hate me forever.

CHAPTER TWENTY-THREE

Golden Prince

I meet Judith Weinstein at the local park where the hippies hang out, and we fall in love during the summer of 1969. I am twenty and uniquely me. She is twenty-three, rich, blonde, smart, popular, and Jewish. Her father is a circuit court judge. She rides a motorcycle, digs the Rolling Stones and Janis Joplin, and is into the LSD scene.

For hours, we discuss the gloom of Vietnam, conspiracy theories surrounding the assassination of John F. Kennedy, Abby Hoffman's idea of dropping LSD in the water supply, and the burning of draft cards. Then we drop acid and make out. Being with Judith is an evangelical experience.

I talk her into meeting with me at the same place the following week. I plan it all out. I bring a blanket, Ripple wine, cheese and crackers, and I spread everything out on the ground in front of the pond so we can watch the ducks.

I want her to like me, so I pluck out fuck songs on the guitar I brought with me, taking my cues from the Stones. She isn't impressed.

The next week I press her to take a drive with me to an out-of-town hiking destination that has a waterfall. I read somewhere that John Donne, a writer of conceited and erotic poems whom I admire, had brilliant success with the ladies.

After we settle onto the blanket, I quote my favorite part of John Donne's love poem Elegy XIX, "To His Mistress Going to Bed."

I finish reading but can't figure out what Judith is thinking. Her expression is blank. "Now that you've heard these words," I say, "I hope you feel the same way I do."

"I don't."

I never speak civilly to Judith again, but thinking about her still makes me hard. I rub myself until I'm on the brink. It never takes long before semen covers my hand.

CHAPTER TWENTY-FOUR

Cinderella

Late at night, I'm awakened. There is no noise, only deathly silence and coldness. I can't move or scream. From the light of the November moon, I can see I'm being cradled by a grinning soldier, but I can't feel him.

I bite my lip, for it isn't without dread that I jump out of bed, rush from my room, and hurry down the hall. At my parents' bedroom door, I raise my hand to knock but then hesitate. We're never supposed to interrupt our parents when they're in their bedroom, but I gather my courage, rap on the door, and call out. "There's someone in my room! Please get him out!"

It takes a long moment for Father to shuffle across the floor and open the door, his face rumpled with sleep. He rubs his eyes, then looks at me questioningly.

"Cinderella," Mother says, rising up on her elbows and turning on the bedside lamp, "you're twelve—much too old for these hysterical outbursts."

"Father, please come," I say, ignoring Mother. I cross the room, pick up his pajama top, and help him put it on. Then he follows me to my room and searches the closet and under the bed.

"No one here, baby girl. You had a bad dream, that's all." He pats my head and returns to his room.

Pacing my bedroom floor, I realize my mind and body are numb. I want nothing more than sleep, but how do I close my eyes at a time like this? As the seconds slowly tick by, my energy trickles away, and I crawl back into bed.

For weeks I can't sleep more than an hour at a time. Strange things happen in the night. I am sick inside and have nowhere to turn. I venture to the back of the house with a flashlight and enter the sanctuary of the trees. I like walking deep into the woods, where the earthy smells are thick and welcoming, unlike the sulfurous odor of boiled eggs that often fills the house. I feel brave in these woods. My brothers have never hurt me here. *How do I go on?* I think as I quietly wait for an answer. But the trees aren't talking.

Mother doesn't see what happens in our family home. She's never seen the soldiers in their tattered uniforms. When I attempt to talk to her, she tells me I'm too sensitive and have an overactive imagination. Mother has a talent for rearranging details in her mind, making them fit snugly into her own perfect world.

CHAPTER TWENTY-FIVE

Pissant

It's a blustery winter day. Father tells me over breakfast that he wants me to carry buckets of wet cement up the ladder to the roof of our three-story house.

"The roof is leaking around the stone chimneys," he says, "and I need you to patch the holes." He digs his knuckles into his lower back. "I'd do it myself, but I've pulled something."

I glance outside at the bending trees. "But won't it be slip-p-pery?"

"Probably, but we've had snow already, and there's more in the forecast. We need to get this done today."

Before we go out, I open Father's liquor cabinet when I'm sure no one is looking. I take a few gulps of scotch, even though I've never grown to like the taste. But I don't mind the bitter sting. Booze short-circuits my stutter and blurs life just the right amount.

Father shouts instructions from the ground, but I do the work up on the roof, carrying shovels of gray goo from the main bucket to the two chimneys. I fill the holes as best I can, but it's not a simple job as rocks have either come loose or fallen out.

As I cross the slick surface, going back and forth to scoop more wet cement, I struggle to avoid slipping on the globs I've already spilled, but the buzz from the scotch makes me woozy. Tripping over my size-twelve feet, I lose my balance and fall.

I'm kept in the hospital for twenty-four hours because of pressure in my head and blurry vision. Then, on Christmas Eve, I'm released with little fanfare, though my parents make a special place for me to sleep in front of the Christmas tree.

For several days I'm sluggish and confused. Although I'm treated specially for the rest of the Christmas break, Golden Prince ribs me about being an uncoordinated klutz. Soon the incident is forgotten, but now it's hard to remember school assignments, and I have little memory of the fall.

CHAPTER TWENTY-SIX

Pissant

In the bathroom mirror, I examine myself with a feeling of profound sadness for what I've lived through. The man on the transistor radio says it January 20, 1970, and there's a deep snow on the way. I've shot up to five-foot-ten and have severe acne. My hair is long, despite Mother's objections, and I wear cool jeans that I purchased myself from a department store.

Every day, I sneak into my parents' liquor cabinet and consume more booze than any fifteen-year-old boy should be able to. I add water to the bottles, hoping Father won't notice the missing ounces. So far, he hasn't.

Our supply of bottles never wanes. At the real estate parties mother attends, particularly over Christmas, people give her fifths of liquor—the good stuff. That's what she says, anyway. She prefers champagne, of course, but Father favors scotch.

From the top shelf of the linen closet, I pull down my hidden bottle of Distiller's Pride. Then I pour the amber fluid into the bathroom water glass. Relishing the burn, I drink it in three gulps.

Choirmaster no longer wants anything to do with me, nor do his friends.

CHAPTER TWENTY-SEVEN

Cinderella

Golden Prince tells me our parents have gone out to celebrate Valentine's Day, and he is to babysit me. It's 1970, and I'm thirteen years old. I object, but it does no good.

Golden Prince says we are going to play hide-and-go-seek and that Pissant is already counting. He claims to know a good hiding spot and wants me to follow him. I do as he says, heading downstairs to the cellar, then into a storage area where I have to stoop to get inside. Wooden shelves stocked with canning jars cover the walls. I don't want to be here doing this, but things will be worse if I don't go along. I look for Wolfdog, but he's not around.

Golden Prince picks up a dirty quilt and tells me to hide under it. Before he does, he snatches my glasses. "Give them back," I say, but he laughs. He knows how badly I need them.

I hear Pissant coming down the basement stairs calling for me. Soon enough, he finds us, and Golden Prince turns off the lights.

I lay in fear, holding back tears as Golden Prince rubs me through my panties before yanking them off. Then it is Pissant's turn to play with me between my legs.

When they are through with me, Golden Prince turns on the overhead light and gives me back my glasses. I am sobbing and can't stop.

"Don't you know this is for your own good?" Golden Prince says. "We're your brothers, and it's up to us to get you ready for future boyfriends. Someday you'll thank us."

"I'll never thank you and will hate you both forever," I say as I crawl across the cellar floor to retrieve my panties. "You are both wicked."

Golden Prince laughs at me.

"I'm s-s-sorry," Pissant says.

"Don't apologize to her," Golden Prince says. "She likes it."

"That's not true, and I wish you both were dead." My anger at least causes my crying to subside. "I want to go upstairs."

"You can't yet," Golden Prince says, reaching out and holding my arm. "I'll tell you when you can."

I know better than to fight back. I stay quiet, hoping he'll forget about me and focus on something else. It doesn't take long.

"Explain again about M-M-Mother and the Ro-Romanov family," Pissant says to our brother.

"Let me smoke this first, and then I'll tell you," Golden Prince says, lighting up a joint. "Either of you want a toke? If you inhale deep, little brother, it will help with your stutter."

I shake my head no, but Pissant puts the joint to his lips, inhales, and coughs. After a few puffs, he grins as if everything is funny.

"In 1917," Golden Prince begins, "Russia was on the verge of collapse because of the revolution. Rasputin, a mystical madman, revealed his vision from God to Nicholas II. He claimed that if he was murdered by nobles, the imperial family would die.

"Soon after, Nicolas abdicated as tsar and was sent into exile with his family. Anastasia was his youngest daughter. They called Anastasia and Milica 'the dark sisters' because they used to hold seances with Rasputin, who was known for the size of his cock and his many lovers.

"European newspapers ran stories that one of Nicholas's daughters may have escaped the firing squad in 1918, thanks to jewels that had been sewn into her clothing for safekeeping. They supposedly blocked the more fatal of the many bullets directed at her.

"Then, in 1920, a woman jumped off a bridge in Berlin. She survived and was taken to a mental institution, where the staff noticed that her scars looked like gunshot wounds. When she finally spoke, she not only had a Russian accent but claimed to be Anastasia.

"Mother thinks Anastasia is her mother because our grandfather, a minister, used to place babies of unwed mothers into suitable homes—and some of those babies came from Europe. Mother believes her parents never told her the truth of her identity, and she's convinced that the wealth of the Romanov family is waiting for her. She just needs to find the proof."

"What kind of p-p-proof?" Second Son says.

"Well, there's Mother's deformed foot, and Anastasia has one too. You've seen the six toes on Mother's left foot, haven't you? She tries to hide it by wearing that special shoe."

"What if it's all true?" I ask, even though I want to get away from my brothers as quickly as I can.

"Then we'll be royalty and very rich." My brothers fall into fits of hysterical laughter. They don't seem to notice as I sneak up the basement stairs.

When I get back to my room, two spiders have built webs in the cracks of my bedroom wall. I feel as if I were the fly caught in my brothers' web today. I watch the spiders, wondering if Sunday School Jesus hides in the cracks and watches me too.

CHAPTER TWENTY-EIGHT

Cinderella

Golden Prince drops his spoon, chipping the edge of Mother's china bowl. Traces of potato soup swirl in his faint mustache.

He turns and glares at me with his icy-blue eyes. But his eyes aren't steady; they search my thirteen-year-old body and face. My heart pounds. I'm frightened of his penetrating stare, of his hands that never stop moving. What does he plan to do to me next?

I shake. Not just my hands, not just my shoulders, but every limb and every muscle. A deep sob erupts from within me as I sit over my TV dinner at the same time that Walter Cronkite announces the date: March 1, 1970.

No one notices my distress except for Golden Prince, who licks his lips in a slow, sexual way and then grins evilly. I want Father to see what Golden Prince is doing and stop him. I need to cling to Father and sob on his shoulder, to tell him the awful things that have been done to me, but he goes on watching TV.

From some tangled place within my heart, a scream erupts, then another. I'm finally heard over the blare of the television. When my final shriek stops, I collapse in my chair. Father rushes to me and puts his hand on my forehead to feel for a temperature.

"She doesn't feel hot, but she is pale," he says to Mother. "Should we call a doctor?"

"No need," Mother says. "Hormones probably. Girls can become hysterical at this age."

Weak from screaming, I implore Father with my eyes. I will him to take charge, to love and protect me. But it's Mother who steers me to my bedroom with Father following.

"Get into bed and wait for me," Mother says. "I'm going to the kitchen to get warm milk."

"I'd like to talk to Father privately," I say, finding the strength to speak, "and for you not to come back in until we're finished."

"Whatever you have to say to your Father, you can say to me,"

Mother says with a look of disapproval. Then she leaves for the kitchen as I get into bed.

"Now don't you worry," Father says from my bedroom door, "everything's going to be all right. Just talk to your mother about what's wrong. I'm sure you'll be fine tomorrow."

His passivity shocks me. *Can't he tell something is wrong with his youngest child—his only daughter?* I want to hit him and yell at him. How could he and Mother not know what happens right under their noses?

For the first time, I realize with profound sadness that my father and I are not only strangers but are destined never to be close. He is not my protector. He doesn't know how to be.

"Drink it all down," Mother coaxes me when she returns and hands me my warm milk.

Defeated, I can do nothing else. I take a few sips, but it numbs my tongue. It takes me only a moment to realize that Mother has put Valium into my drink.

To my parents I am a small brown bird that has flown full speed into a window of glass and—stunned—fallen to the ground.

CHAPTER TWENTY-NINE

Pissant

On May 4, 1970, the Ohio National Guard guns down four students at Kent State University in a hail of sixty-seven shots. Being an advocate for drugs, sex, and rock-and-roll, I can't get my head around blood on campus sidewalks.

I am reminded of John Lennon and Yoko chanting, "Give peace a chance!" on television, and I keep replaying it in my mind.

I light a joint and try to grasp the situation, but it does no good. Darkness and light have taken hold of the world, and the Beatles have broken up.

CHAPTER THIRTY

Cinderella

I try to be more like Luke. While at the stables, I smile and pretend to be a confident teen, not a thirteen-year-old girl who lives at the mercy of her brothers.

One beautiful October day, I walk into Chestnut's stall, and she whinnies a greeting. Whenever we're together, I don't wallow in my failures. For Chestnut's sake, I let go of my tension. Usually, after the first few minutes in her company, I can. I've learned already that it is foolish to be impatient with her, and it's cruel to withhold affection. I respect her too much.

"Chestnut needs you to touch her the way her mother would," Luke says with his southern drawl.

I don't remember Mother ever touching or holding me in a

loving way, but I caress Chestnut, giving her lots of reassuring touches and hugs around her neck. I love it when she relaxes, yawns, licks her lips, and gives me soft taps with her nose.

"Ready to ride?" Luke says. "I've picked out a gentle path through the woods. Today, I'll follow you. It won't be long before you can go out on your own."

"Sounds great," I say, excited about this development. "Chestnut and I are ready to go." The day is brisk, the golden leaves are falling, and Mother won't be back for several hours. It doesn't get any better than this.

Luke rarely talks much, but when he does, I listen. Today is one of those days.

"Chestnut understands what you want her to do and is smart enough to think through situations. Horses have a lot to teach us if we let them. When I was comin' up, my father stayed drunk a lot of the time and used to push us all around—my mother, my little sister, and me. Things got pretty bad, as you can imagine. So bad that when I was fourteen, my mother took off with my sister." I hear a catch in his throat, but I don't dare turn around to see. "Guess she figgered I was old enough to take care of myself by then. And who knows? Maybe I was. I've not seen them since, but I wish them well. I guess what I'm tryin' to say is, horses saved me."

"I'm sorry, Luke," I say, not knowing what else to offer.

"Everyone has demons. All we can do is focus on what's happenin' right now. You look at the trail ahead, not the dust and footprints you've left behind. That's the best that any of us can do."

I don't tell Luke what goes on in my house. I am too ashamed. Chestnut is the only relationship I want or need.

* * *

School is hard. It's 1971, and I've started the ninth grade. I wish I were quick like the other students, but I'm a slow learner, even if no one comes out and says it. Two of my teachers taught Golden Prince, so they know that some family potential exists, but they also taught Pissant, who only made passing grades and had to work hard for those. In my case, even with diligent studying, Ds and Fs fill my report card. I can tell that my teachers feel sorry for me; they no longer look for that familial spark of genius.

After school one afternoon, I pull the wooden basement door open with a squeak and drag the laundry basket across the floor to the washing machine. When I hear Pissant behind me, I freeze, afraid to move a muscle, not knowing what he is about to do. He turns me around and brushes my long brown hair back from my face.

"Stop!" I yell. "Don't ever touch me again! I know Golden Prince put you up to it, but you should never have gone along. You're both rapists!"

"I p-p-promise I won't t-t-touch you," Pissant says as tears fall down his pale, gaunt face. "I a-a-a-pologize for what I did. It was... wrong... and I'll never do it again. I kn-know what it feels like to be... hurt by people you-you-you should be able to trust."

I stand there speechless as he continues to speak. He offers to teach me to sing, thinking I might like the high school choir as much as he does. But I can't sing, and I have no talent or desire. If I'm honest, there are no extracurricular activities I'm suited for. Even if there were, they're certainly not encouraged at home, at least not for me.

I'd like nothing more than to be like the other kids at school, walking hand-in-hand, being in love, talking of summer beach trips, going steady, holding down future jobs, and maybe even going to college, but I'll never be like the cheerleaders, who go to football games and flirt, and I'll certainly never date a jock.

The future sorority types snicker and make fun of me, even to my face. At least the hippies on the smoking block, where I hang out, are never mean to me. All they seem interested in is getting stoned, going to the drive-in, and screwing. A few of them are good at art, but that isn't me either. I use drugs, preferring whatever I can smoke or snort; maybe that's my talent.

The nights are the worst. I wake up racking with sobs because of my dreams. I know I'll never go back to sleep, so I climb out my bedroom window. I stay out as long as I dare, drifting mentally and physically from place to place. Eventually I end up in the woods behind the house talking to Wolfdog. *Tell me boy, why do I like these woods? Did something happen here?* Wolfdog usually lies down beside me. He never answers.

My life has no point. I go on living because that's what my body is used to doing. I wait for someone to save me, but no one comes. Thankfully, I have Chestnut and Wolfdog.

CHAPTER THIRTY-ONE

Pissant

Late at night, I lie in bed with my ear pressed to my transistor radio as I ask questions of my Magic 8-Ball. Mother is doing so well in real estate that she no longer rents out rooms in our house. Now that I'm a junior in high school, I finally have a room of my own.

My looks have gotten better although I wear glasses. I'm not fat, but I'm not muscular, and I suck at sports. I'm the awkward guy who plays the trombone in the high school band—something I at least seem to have a gift for.

I read in the September issue of *Rolling Stone* that on October 12, 1971, *Jesus Christ Superstar*, the rock opera by Andrew Lloyd Webber, will open on Broadway. I get really excited when the high school band director says he is taking us to New York over Thanksgiving break to see it.

Finally, the big day arrives. The bus trip is long but well worth it. We do the regular sightseeing—Statue of Liberty and Empire State Building—even though it's November and absolutely freezing. I am so excited to be in New York. I love the smell of the roasted chestnuts and eat several hotdogs from the vendor carts on the sidewalks. Everything here is bigger than life, nothing like back home. Back at the hotel, we get ready for our night at the theater.

I sit on the edge of my seat when the play begins. I'm a little high on pot but not too far gone. The music and costumes enthrall me. But more than that, I feel an immediate connection to the Judas character when he comes on stage. After he says his first lines, I know we share tormented minds. He betrayed Jesus; I betrayed my sister. The play wakes up my soul. I'll never be the same. My stuttering stops.

After we get home from New York, I listen to Bob Dylan's "With God on Our Side" over and over, memorizing the last two verses. I practice picking it out on the guitar. After a while, I sound almost as good as Dylan.

I particularly like the lines where Jesus is betrayed by a kiss, and when Dylan warbles that if God was on his side, He'd stop the next war.

Is God on the side of me and my sister? What about the Vietnam War—which side there? Better yet, is God on the side of Choirmaster and his friends? I have so many questions but no answers. Not yet anyway.

CHAPTER THIRTY-TWO

Cinderella

An artificial tinsel tree stands in the living room. My father smiles, showing his tombstone teeth and saying that Santa's elves brought the tree and covered it in glitter. That stuff worked when I was a little girl, but I know it's the same tree we've used year after year, just like the cheap plastic wreaths on the door and the blow-up Santa Claus in the front yard. It is 1971 after all.

On Christmas Eve, my parents start out drinking eggnog, then switch to champagne. The newspaper reports that after thirty-two years, the German Supreme Court has ended the case of Anastasia. They cannot prove that the woman who claims to be Anastasia is an imposter.

"Let's raise a glass and celebrate the news!" Mother says. "I'm a step closer to being a rightful heir." She pours champagne for all of us, and we give her a cheer. "I have a mind to call the television reporters and have them interview me."

"I think you should meet your mother in person first," Father says, "before jumping the gun. You'll need all your ducks in a row before they'll listen to you."

"You're right, of course, but I have a feeling it won't be long now!" Mother says with a smile. "Let's all settle down and enjoy the blaze in the fireplace. It's made the room so warm and cozy."

My parents hold hands. Presents sit under the tree. Golden Prince plays Mozart and Bach on the piano. Good smells, lingering in the air from the sugar cookies I baked and decorated this afternoon, waft toward us from the kitchen. It feels like what a Christmas should, for a short while anyway.

That night we open our gifts. Second Son gets the trombone he's been asking for, and Golden Prince receives money, though I don't know how much. I receive clothes as I usually do. Mother is more concerned with the way I look, not how I am.

Golden Prince hands me a wrapped package. He's never given me a Christmas present before. I open the box and find a blue monarch butterfly pressed between two thin panes of glass. Horrified, I jump up, scream, and then sob, not understanding why I'm reacting this way. But I do know that once again, Golden Prince has put something vile inside my soul: a beautiful dead monarch that will taint my life from that day forward. For I am that butterfly. But no one understands, least of all me.

CHAPTER THIRTY-THREE

Cinderella

On January 15, 1972, I turn fifteen and my parents give me a Polaroid camera and film for my birthday. For dinner we have fried chicken, which Mother actually makes. Our family sits in the living room, eating off of TV trays as usual. A special cake, chocolate with buttercream frosting, sits in the center of the coffee table. I blow out the candles and make a silent wish for Golden Prince not to hurt me anymore

Afterward, when I take the plates to the kitchen, Golden Prince grabs me from behind, and I wet my pants.

That night, I sit in the bathtub, scrubbing. I'm dirty... dirty... dirty...

Later that night in my room, I rock back and forth, unable to sleep and not trusting that one of my rapist brothers—or both—will climb into my bed.

* * *

Daily I find our house to be alive and watchful, and when the soldiers come near, blood surges in my ears. I sense their approach and hear their faint singing:

> Till the war is over
> I'll join the bloody strife
> My spirit will not falter
> For I'm a Southern soldier.

Wolfdog is always with me when they come.

I take pictures inside the house with my Polaroid camera, capturing strange orbs that emit shimmering green, yellow, and orange lights. I don't understand what they are, but they're beautiful. I hide my camera from Golden Prince. He wants to take pictures of me without my clothes on, but I will never let that happen.

One morning I wake suddenly, as if being nudged. I hear my name being called, but there is no one in my room or at my door. Still, Wolfdog paces around my bed, seeming to demand my attention. Given my usual gray and struggling mood upon waking, I want only to settle back onto my lumpy pillow, but Wolfdog refuses to let that happen. Reluctantly, I get out of bed and head downstairs.

When I enter the living room, a book falls to the floor from the mantel over the fireplace. I bend over and pick it up to see that it is a journal containing regimental histories. A list of names fills many pages. An odor of tobacco and leather lingers in the air. *What do the soldiers want me to know?* I ask the journal but it remains silent.

Weeks pass and my brothers don't come near me. I believe the Confederate soldiers and Wolfdog are keeping them away, but I might be wrong.

* * *

I think of things Luke has said to me during my riding lessons. He's more than a teacher; he's my friend, even though at thirty he's twice my age. Best of all, he has set Mother straight on my riding clothes, so now I look like everyone else.

Early on, Mother said she'd refuse to pay for my riding lessons if I didn't wear the ridiculous outfits she'd chosen, but I told her I wouldn't ride in shows and compete. Luckily, Luke came to my rescue.

"I pass your house on my way to the stables," he said to Mother. "I can pick your daughter up and return her. For two Saturdays a month, she'll be my employee, and I'll pay her with lessons."

Mother, eager for me to maintain the equestrian connections she assumed I was making, reluctantly agreed.

Now, after my lessons, I clean out stalls, and then I'm free to trail-ride. Sometimes Luke comes with me, sometimes not.

On one sun-drenched July day, Chestnut and I head out through the towering pines, where I always feel like a character in a fairy tale. The green tendrils and wildflowers make me think of wood nymphs and sprites. I smile. Are they hiding in the woods? I like to think so. In the forest, the temperature is cooler but still plenty hot, and I'm glad I brought a canteen of water.

Riding over a spongy carpet of pine needles, I cross Barking Creek. A gigantic fallen oak, split by lightning and hollowed by age, lies on the ground. I wonder which animals shelter there—snakes, squirrels, rabbits? Chestnut and I continue for another hour before stopping to eat the lunch I packed and carried in a brown paper bag. I also have an apple and sugar cubes for Chestnut.

"Here you are, girl," I say, feeding her the juicy red fruit. When she finishes, I remount and we head back to the stables. "I'll give you the sugar cubes when we finish our ride, Chestnut."

We are halfway back when a summer storm comes in fast. Icy chills run through me. There's no place to shelter and wait it out, but we are near the fallen oak. I tie Chestnut's reins around a tall pine and tell her that everything will be okay. Then, curling into a fetal position, I snuggle into the tree and protect myself as best I can.

Thunder shakes the woods, and darkness covers the path. The rain beats down like small hammers on my arms and legs, biting into my flesh.

Finally the storm passes, and, as if out of nowhere, a surreal feeling overwhelms me. The shame and grief that have lived in my heart for so long are gone. My fear disappears and I feel freer than I ever have. I stop shuddering and slowly uncurl my body. A rainbow arcs over the woods.

In the deepest part of me, I know how to survive.

PART TWO

I seemed to have loved you

In numerous forms,

Numerous times...

In life after life,

In age after age,

Forever...

~ Rabindranath Tagore

CHAPTER THIRTY-FOUR

Pissant

It's the summer of 1972, and I've graduated from high school. I'm six-foot-two with muttonchops and a mustache. Attending a festival in the park, I listen to the Swinging Kings perform. I'm blown away by their big-band music and how they play the songs of Three Dog Night and Blood, Sweat & Tears. When they finish their first set, I get up my nerve, approach the band, and introduce myself.

"I know this might be bragging," I say to the lead singer, "but I've been told I play a mean trombone. Could I play for you sometime?"

"Do you have something prepared? I'm Mac, and this is my band."

"Yeah, as a matter of fact I do, but I didn't bring my instrument with me."

"You can borrow the one we've got, and since it's break, the stage is all yours." He gestures to the raised platform. "Let's see what've you got."

I climb up, take a few deep breaths, then let loose with Glenn Miller's "In The Mood." It doesn't take long before people are grooving to the music of my borrowed trombone.

This is the moment I've been waiting for my entire life.

I'm invited to audition. I pay for a Beatles haircut and cuffed jeans, wanting to look like the other band members. I endlessly practice the rock ballads and specialty songs that the Swinging Kings played at the park. When my big day comes, I perform with everything I have.

"You're pretty good, kid," Mac says. "Tell you what I'll do. You can rehearse with us for a couple of weeks. Then I'll let you know."

"If I didn't tell you," I say, "I can sing too."

Mac wears an enormous grin when I finish belting out "With God On Our Side." Before I know it, I'm part of the band.

111

The guys have played together for several years. Three of them are twenty-two, and Mac is twenty-six. I'm the youngest and take a lot of ribbing, like a lovable mascot. Mac gives me a few solo parts at college dances and country club events, and I like that we wear matching shirts, vests, or tuxedos, depending on the gig. More important than that, girls are noticing me.

Trying to fit in, I mix a full bottle of grain alcohol with grape Kool-Aid, making a punch we call Screaming Purple Jesus to drink after the shows. What the guys don't finish, I do. They always drive me home, and my parents are still asleep when I enter the house. I'm often still drunk the next morning.

Amber, with long blonde hair, follows the band and sometimes brings her friends. One night I get up my nerve, light my cigarette, and, after a deep drag, go over to talk to her.

We down a couple cups of Screaming Purple Jesus and talk about Bob Dylan, Mick Jagger, and Joan Baez. Then she has to go because her friends are waiting. That's always the way it is.

CHAPTER THIRTY-FIVE

Cinderella

Its January 1973, and Mother insists I attend real estate parties with her as she looks for big investors. I don't enjoy these events and resent being paraded around while Mother puts together deals, like turning run-down motels into public housing on the edge of town. I'm her chauffeur, having gotten my learner's permit, and often drive her home after her nights out.

At these parties, the booze flows as Perry Como and Robert Goulet play from the stereo speakers. People dance, laugh, and sometimes pass out. The real estate market is booming as city dwellers flee their high-rises and move to the suburbs—Mother's suburbs, as she sees it.

"I can't take your father to these affairs," Mother complains. "He's always pulling out pictures of the Arabians when I'm trying to close transactions. He demands way too much attention for himself. Plus, it's better if you're here because one of these agents might have a son your age."

"I don't think that's going to happen here, Mother. Most of your friends are partying, and the last thing they want to think about is their kids. You mingle while I find the ladies' room." I walk away from Mother in search of a cocktail. What she doesn't know won't hurt her. It doesn't take me long to find a bottle of Jack Daniels and some cola in the kitchen. I mix a drink and down it quickly, thinking about the real reasons Mother doesn't want Father here.

Mother is embarrassed by Father's looks and what he wears. I've overheard many of their arguments. She buys him new shirts and pants from the sale rack and picks out his outfits for events. But Father won't wear them, insisting that his worn and dated clothes are good enough. He resents Mother trying to change him and has told her so. Seems to me they've reached a stalemate on that issue as well as others.

Once tall, Father is now stooped, his dyed red hair showing white at the temples. His skin gives off a grayish tinge, and the shadows beneath his eyes look like bruises. When he climbs steps, he becomes winded and complains of a tightness in his chest, yet he refuses to see a doctor.

Mother, on the other hand, doesn't see how much she differs from the more stylish real estate agents. If it's winter, she wears the musty fur coat she purchased from a thrift store and, more often than not, she has a run in her stocking. After several glasses of champagne, her reapplied lipstick looks like smeared jam.

I fix myself another cocktail and nibble on peanuts that have been left on the counter, then notice I am not alone. A good-looking older man is watching me, and I feel dirty under his gaze. Smiling, he moves in my direction. Once he has his arm around me, he brags that one of his daughters is in training at the Barbizon Modeling School in New York. Then he asks me to go to the bedroom with him because he has pictures of her in his briefcase there. It isn't long before we're having sex under the guests' coats.

Prince Charming doesn't show up when I'm with Mother at these parties. Nor does my lost slipper.

* * *

A month after the January cocktail party with Mother, I'm left barefoot in a back alley after a night of drinking with high-school boys, whose names and faces I can't remember. My period doesn't come.

For days, I don't eat and can't sleep, so I spend time in the basement away from the others. While on my knees, I plead and bargain with Sunday School Jesus. I tell Him I won't have sex again if He will keep this pregnancy from happening. How can I ever have a baby with brothers like mine? And I'd be a shitty mother too.

My mind spins with the consequences of my poor decisions. I hoard enough rage, guilt, and sorrow to fill the hundreds of overflowing trash bags in our house. Yet I can't stop my painful memories from coming; I examine them one by one. Who has sex with their brothers—and with anyone else who wants to? Why have I never been able to say no? I tell myself I have to forget things, that forgetting is the only way to survive, but I feel like a candle sputtering in the dark.

Another month passes. I'm at school when the cramping starts. I excuse myself from English class and rush to the bathroom. Sitting on the toilet bowl, I spread my legs and see a clear mucus blob with a red tinge bobbing in the water. It's unmistakable what it is. I reach into the toilet bowl, scoop my hand under it, and bring it to my face for a closer look. I cry and cannot stop. Not knowing what to do, I reach in my pocket for a Kleenex and wrap up the wet bloody mess as best I can. There is no way I'll flush my unwanted baby into the sewage system. Please, Sunday School Jesus, forgive me, and thank you for answering my prayer.

I leave school without permission, crying so hard that I stumble into the road, then drag myself to a nearby park. By the creek, I pick up a sharp rock and, with all the strength I have, dig a hole with its edges. I put the Kleenex in the hole and cover it with dirt and stones. Then I bow my head and say a prayer for this small creature that never was.

CHAPTER THIRTY-SIX

Bastard Man

Golden Prince makes a deal with his mother that he will continue to work for her if she'll finance a house for him with a low mortgage rate. Until this year, 1973, he's been in no hurry to move out. His room has its own entrance through a side porch, and he comes and goes as he pleases, all while eating our food. His bedroom, with his hundreds of books, is the best room in the house.

When his moving day comes, I do the heavy lifting. He wants to take everything from his room as well as furniture and decorative items that Anastasia said he could have. Finally, at twenty-three, he is out of his childhood home and officially moved into an old two-story house near the university. He's never really worked a day in his life. By the time I was his age,

I'd graduated from college, worked a job, married his mother, and had him.

I'm glad he's gone, although I'd never say so to Anastasia. She worships the boy. I don't. He thinks he's better and smarter than me, often directing condescending sneers my way. The older he gets, the more he reminds me of my adoptive father, a true jackass if ever there was one.

Within weeks, Golden Prince rents out rooms to college students, particularly girls. This pays his mortgage and gives him spending cash, but I notice that none of the students stay for long. I don't know the details—not that he'd share them with me—but I hear things through Anastasia that I wish she'd keep to herself.

Cinderella wants his room, but Anastasia says no because she might want to find a tenant for it. I say let the girl have it, but my wishes fall on deaf ears. It's not an argument I can win, so I don't try. I understand little about these children I've sired, or about my wife.

A month after moving Golden Prince into his house, I walk into the barbershop and hear two men laughing about Pissant. When they see me, they stop talking. For a long time, I've suspected my son is a homosexual, always figuring that's how he got the nickname. But I don't want to know anything about it. I knew of some queers while growing up, and I saw how people snickered and carried on about it. Maybe it's something Pissant will outgrow.

In particular, I remember going into the barn and seeing my adoptive father's real son having sex with an older teenager. I didn't know such things were possible between males. At ten, I knew how farm animals mated, but not much of anything else. Seemed like whenever my adoptive father was away on business, my so-called brother had friends over. I sure made myself scarce when he did, often taking one of the beagles into the woods to chase rabbits.

It's nothing short of a miracle I'm married to Anastasia. Every night I thank my lucky stars that she looked at me twice. Anastasia takes care of all the details with the Arabians, the business, and our children. Hopefully, she'll steer Pissant in the right direction. I'm along for the ride. I'd like to have a dog, but Anastasia says no.

CHAPTER THIRTY-SEVEN

Pissant

The counters are littered with dishes and silverware, and the pots on the stove are unwashed and full of grease. A box fan blows in the doorway.

When I enter the kitchen to get orange juice, I see Cinderella carrying dishes from last night's dinner trays into the kitchen. It's going to be a scorching July day, breaking records for 1973. At least that's what the radio says.

For a moment Cinderella stands still after setting the dishes down, her hands hanging idly at her sides. All her senses seem stretched as she gazes out the kitchen window. "Somewhere among the trees, he's waiting for you," she says.

"Who's waiting for me?"

"What?" she says, turning to me. A moment later, her brain seems to clear. "I don't know why I said that."

Outside, the trees do seem to stand still, as if waiting for me to speak. "I've said it before, Cinderella, but I'm sorry I hurt you. Do you think you'll ever forgive me?"

She stops for a few seconds, then looks into my eyes. "I know why they call you Pissant. Golden Prince told me the sordid details about what Choirmaster and his friends did to you. He says you liked it, but I don't believe him. Maybe I don't hate you after all."

I feel a tremendous relief when she tells me this. My sister doesn't hate me anymore!

That day, just before dusk, the thunder growls, and a quick downpour of rain cools the Earth. When the weather clears, I walk to the park and slip LSD under my tongue, compliments of Mac, my band leader.

Within minutes, a golden-pink flush spreads across the sky, and the trees lift their arms in worship while shrilling birds sound out their happiness. The world is putting on colors and shapes just for me.

I am transparent, clairvoyant, and the night contains all things.

I feel a rooted, wonderful joy, and I weep with a sense of release and lighthearted playfulness.

A marble statue of Pan, surrounded by pink hydrangeas and red roses, beckons me. Pan smiles and lifts his flute, playing a haunting melody while he dances. The fragrance of the magnificent Aphrodite titillates my senses and I know that she too is here. I want to be Pan, and for a while I am. I am no longer the forgotten middle child, abused by many. That night I am one with Pan and believe in God.

CHAPTER THIRTY-EIGHT

Cinderella

I'm a sophomore in high school and I preen, hoping a boy—any boy—will like me. I keep my lips wet with gloss and take black beauties to overcome my shyness and desire to eat. I find it funny that my drug of choice is named after a famous horse. Vodka softens the harshness of my world when I come down from speed. I'm a slow undertow that's quietly wild.

Volatile and inconsistent, I do badly in school. I spend my time on the smoking block and turn to ludes when I can get them. Most of the students are looking forward to the summer break, but not me. Summers are endless days of hell, caught at home. Why can't I change for the better? After I was caught in the storm with Chestnut, I felt unequivocally that I was strong enough to survive anything. But so much has happened to me since then. My bravado has been chipped away by loneliness and despair. Yet I hold out hope that a little of it remains in me somewhere.

By junior year, I wear my dull brown hair in a ponytail, and my fingernails are bitten to the quick. My dealer, a Vietnam vet, gets busted, but it's no problem for me to score pot. A blow job in the school parking lot usually gets me some good hash.

Trapped in my head with images that won't stop, I no longer care how I look. My brothers fed me only brokenness while feasting on my flesh. I've lived nothing but shit.

Picking up a pair of scissors from Mother's sewing kit, I butcher my greasy locks. With an acne-pitted face, hairy legs, and the scale hitting 230 pounds, my brothers don't bother with me anymore.

I graduate from high school in 1976. It has taken me an extra year. It's sweltering hot for June, yet I'm cold and shivering inside. Mosquitoes have bitten me all over, and I scratch until I draw blood. Covering myself with a dark gray blanket, my bed becomes my world. Nothing in life makes sense.

I'm pregnant again and have no idea who the father is. I've probably been with a dozen guys at different rock festivals. It's supposed to be all about free love, drugs, and rock-and-roll, but then why do I feel so guilty and empty inside? Enough is enough. No one will ever use my body again. *Yeah, right.* I've broken my promise to Sunday School Jesus more times than I can count.

I get the name of a doctor who performs abortions, and I plan to have my tubes tied at the same time. Since I'm nineteen, I don't need a parent's permission. In 1973, the Supreme Court legalized the procedure, so at least I won't be having it done in a back alley. Regardless, I don't want my family to know; it's none of their business.

Since I don't have any money, I rummage through Mother's jewelry box. Most of her stuff is costume, but she has a few expensive pieces. All of it is in a huge, jumbled mess, so I untangle several rings and take them to the pawnshop. Mother won't notice anything is missing.

The abortion and sterilization procedures are performed coldly and efficiently. On the slim chance that I ever get pregnant again, I'll kill myself. There's no way I'll bring a child, especially a girl, into this world, and I'll never abort another child. Wolfdog and Chestnut are all I have, and that has to be enough.

* * *

A few days after the abortion, I'm up early again because I don't sleep well. I go to the kitchen and make coffee. I don't notice Wolfdog crossing the dirty floor until he looks up and searches my face. Wolfdog allows me my wicked thoughts and never judges.

After drinking my coffee, I put my dirty clothes into the washing machine. Wolfdog follows. I clean the kitchen while the laundry finishes, and when it's done, I carry the basket of wet clothes out the back door to hang on the line. Again, Wolfdog follows. It's unusual for him to stay so close.

Later that afternoon, while changing my sheets, I hear a faint voice or moan coming from somewhere. There isn't anyone else in the house, is there? I venture to the living room to be near the front door in case an intruder is hiding upstairs. Standing still, I listen for more sounds from either the street or the house. Why am I suddenly afraid?

When I turn my gaze to the staircase, soldiers are staring down on me. My eyes dart about for an easy escape, but my feet feel glued in place. The boy soldiers—for they look too young to be called men—descend the stairs and saunter to the parlor, except for one, who remains on the bottom step.

This soldier stares at me, as if searching for a resemblance or a kind word.

I swipe at my eyes. What can I say that he will understand? He reaches a ghost hand out to me, and I stand frozen, unable to move.

Footsteps suddenly sound out behind me, gaining speed, getting closer, then banking harder as if marching. Panic sweeps through me, and the ghost soldier pulls his hand away.

The soldiers disappear into the walls and after they do, I pull the outer door tight. Peering through a side window, I watch them trot behind our house, along a path deep with dust.

For hours, I sit at the kitchen table, flooded with memories of a blue dress with a white sash tied at the waist. I am a ghost, and I'm not even dead.

* * *

For days, it rains. I gaze out the window as I peel the dinner potatoes over the sink. I'm twenty years old and have no plans for my life. How did I let this happen?

As I watch the shadows of the trees, I sense Confederate soldiers pulsing through the floorboards. They want me to know they're there.

No one would care if I vanish from the earth, except maybe Moon Woman, a palm reader I meet at a bookstore while buying tarot cards.

"Let's sit outside at one of the café tables," she says, "and I'll read the cards for you. Don't worry about my usual charge. This reading is my gift to you."

As we talk, her face assumes an expression of yearning and seems to float upward to the moon. Then she closes her eyes and speaks with a dreamy clairvoyance. As she does, blood throbs in my ears, and my mouth goes dry.

"The little girl that once was you is lost," she says. "I can help you get her safely back into your body, but it will take work."

"What do I need to do?"

"For now, take these three pink prayer candles"—she pulls them from her purse—"and pray to your guardian angels. I'll teach you how."

Week after week I meet with Moon Woman, paying whatever she asks. Sometimes she takes the money but other times she refuses.

Mother can't stop me from seeing her, no matter how hard she tries.

"I'm going, and there's nothing you can do," I say. "And you're paying for it too. I've lived on your slave wages long enough."

Moon Woman becomes my trusted friend and spiritual advisor. She is my measuring rod. For twenty years I've had no way to assess myself, but with her I can.

* * *

One evening, after a transcendental meditation class with Moon Woman, the Confederate soldier from the stairway stands in the shadow of my bedroom door. Giving me a toothy grin, he whistles a tune. I'm afraid to look at him, so I turn my back and face the dresser's mirror.

To my horror, my image shows in the soldier's eyes, and an odd sensation passes through my body. I'm hollow inside except for him, and a swarm of buzzing bees fills my head. The experience quickly passes but leaves a surprisingly sweet taste of honey in my mouth. Maybe he means me no harm.

The next morning, due to either depression or exhaustion, I don't get up until noon. When I do, the first thing that comes to mind is the solider. Again I look into the mirror. *Was he real?*

The mirror says nothing in return but does reflect my confusion.

I halfheartedly brush my hair and get dressed. Then I leave the house and walk the two miles to the bookstore. Upon entering, I see Moon Woman at a table drinking a cup of tea. Rising from her chair, she lifts her arms and softly and gently encircles me.

"You're crying," she says.

"I'm afraid."

"You've had a vision, and this is good."

CHAPTER THIRTY-NINE

Cinderella

I go to the cellar in search of canning jars. I've seen them scattered amongst the discarded items left behind by those who lived here before us. I plan to put white candles in the beautiful blue jars and place them around my room. We've never had a garden, much less canned food of any kind, but it's something I want to try. There's an energy about the blue hue that I love, and Moon Woman thinks it's a good idea.

Moon Woman gives me nutritional guidance, which I have followed to the letter. I feel so much better, having lost thirty pounds in the last six months, and I sit in zazen meditation daily. At first it was agony, but after a few weeks, with regular practice, I increase my sitting time to thirty minutes a day. My life has improved with Moon Woman's help.

From the cellar's wooden shelves, I pull at least a hundred canning jars, mostly clear but a few blue. A surprising amount contain rotten food, which I hastily discard. After I've removed all of them, I shine my flashlight against the back wall, where I spy loose stones. Noticing something odd behind one of the stones, I reach for and pull out a small book wrapped in tattered strips of blue and gray, most likely from old garments.

Upstairs, I carefully remove the strips that cover the book, grateful that no one else is home. With trembling hands, I open to the cover page, fearful that the ragged tome might fall apart. I see a dedication page and start to read, forgetting why I'd originally gone to the cellar.

CHAPTER FORTY

The Journal

I dedicate this journal to

Miss Susan Meador

14 Washington Street

Lexington, Virginia

April 2, 1862

My Dearest Susan,

Standing on your doorstep intent on a heartfelt goodbye, I had hope in my heart. I am convinced you have strong feelings for me, for you could not hide your bottom lip from quivering or the single tear that fell from your eye.

Political matters loom dark, with scarcely a ray of light. Your father aims to be VMI's next college president, and my father opposes every Southern ideal that your father holds sacred. Yet despite my namesake's beliefs, I know it is my duty to protect my homeland.

You spoke of your mother's persistent hollow cough and your duty as the youngest daughter to live at home and care for her and the household. I hope she is improving.

I am beyond distressed to hear that your father forbade you further contact with me because of the hardened, chilled, and stubborn impressions made between our families. I cannot tell you how much I regret your decision not to write or receive my correspondence. It wounds me more greatly than any bullet ever could, and I pray that the great gulf between us will one day be passable, for you and I are victims of a strange destiny.

It seems I am to be Romeo, and you my Juliet.

Thomas Divers

Pissant and Cinderella

May 1, 1862

My Dearest Susan,

I remember with such fondness the day of the church social and the laughter we shared during our great butterfly chase and while playing with my Irish wolfhound.

When I secured the prize of the blue monarch, which I placed on your shoulder like a glittering bauble, you allowed me a gentle kiss. This cherished memory is how I shall remember you for always.

Homer (my dog, not the writer—I jest) has followed me. There seems no way to make him go home, so I read him what I write to you.

My highest earthly desire, as I lay in the trenches with my dog and other Virginia homegrown boys and gaze at the starry sky, is to gain your unlimited love.

Your one and only,

Thomas

July 1, 1862

My Dearest Susan,

I fought with General Joseph E. Johnston seven miles from our capital. Our losses were enormous and Johnston maimed. I took a shot in the left shoulder but shall survive.

When the shooting ceased, my comrades, faint from thirst, praised Homer, who had run toward the enemy, discovered a pool of water, then rushed back and loudly announced it with his barks. He shows an understanding of what we need and does his best to help.

Remembering today is your eighteenth birthday, I cannot help but reflect on a vision of you in your favorite blue dress and the picnic we shared by the creek, where I held your hand in mine. These memories help me go on.

Yours truly,

Thomas

December 25, 1862

My Dearest Susan,

Although you can offer me only a tender friendship, it is my forever hope you will change your mind and upon my return say "yes" to my desire for marriage. Without you, my love shall stay buried in a battleground, and I shall never care for another.

Since following me, Homer has grown faster than a lion and proven to be courageous, humble, and fierce at catching chickens and squirrels. He brings them back to me, and I share them with the other soldiers, thus supplementing our rations. How I pity the poor dogs that have been left at home awaiting their masters.

I send my fondest wishes and pray I shall see you in my dreams.

On this the day of our Lord and Savior's birth,

Thomas

Linda Kay Simmons

February 7, 1863

My Dearest Susan,

It was the coldest of nights when, by luck, three of us who were scouting ahead came across a deserted barn. As I slept in a haystack with Homer, in desperate need of rest and warmth, I was awakened to the sensation of Homer rising and charging from the barn. He barked furiously, then howled like a wolf. I rose as fast as I could and spied him with an arch in his back, baring his teeth, though I was unable to spy an enemy.

I alerted my comrades, who rose quickly. Then the three of us stole silently into the night.

Within minutes, four horsemen in Union uniforms dismounted and searched the barn. We took them by surprise. At sunrise, we found a peaceful place under the pines and dug their graves. Daniel, the oldest of us, spoke a verse he remembered from childhood, wanting to thank Homer for saving our lives:

"Over the hill and 'cross the level, Thomas's wolfdog treed the devils."

After covering the Union soldiers with dirt, I said a silent prayer for their souls, and we went on our way.

I wished I'd had a buttermilk biscuit to give Homer, for he likes them almost as much as he likes me.

With love,

Thomas

Linda Kay Simmons

March 4, 1863

My Dearest Susan,

Today is the second anniversary of the inauguration of Lincoln. Rumors of disaster and defeat have reached my ears and are deplorable if true.

My days lengthen into weeks, then weeks into months. Still you refuse to write. A letter from you would feel like an angel's visit and dispel my gloom.

I am heartened that Homer is with me. He lifts the men's morale. Another of the men has his coonhound with him. He and Homer hunt possum, rushing after smells in the night woods.

With my pocketknife, I am whittling my faithful dog's likeness into a piece of golden oak. It helps to pass the time.

Yours forever,

Thomas Divers

July 7, 1863

My Dearest Susan,

Yesterday I turned twenty, and my thoughts are lighter, having had two full days' rest. At last, my stomach is sated from many a shot rabbit.

For my birthday, a comrade played his banjo, while another the harmonica, and we danced and sang "Dixie" with all of the men joining in on "I wish I was in Dixie, Hooray! Hooray!" You never could imagine such a sight as us.

Homer, my frolicking creature, jumped on me, knocking me down with his love. How I wished it had been you!

I pray for the day when I shall hold you again—and let our fathers be damned!

Your one and only,

Thomas

September 6, 1863

My Beloved Susan,

I had confidence in our generals, but they have abused my trust. Sickness has taken hold, and they have left several men on the side of the road.

There are many signs of trouble, but I do not wish to write about battles, mangled bodies, heroes, and deserters. It is only by the grace of God I have survived.

In the words of Homer the poet: "By their own follies they perished, the fools."

Yours forever,

Thomas Divers

January 23, 1864

My Dearest Susan,

This winter is viciously cold. We survive on meager rations, and only a few of us have shoes. Homer, with his rough and hard white coat and his strong instinct to hunt, chases deer and other creatures, returning with a squirrel or rabbit he's shaken by the neck, even dragging a deer back to camp on one feast-laden night.

I have been without pen and ink in which to scrawl my thoughts to you. Sadly, the death of a comrade now allows me to correspond again.

An eye infection left me incapacitated for weeks, but I am improved. More men than can be imagined have been maimed or killed in skirmishes, while others have gone missing. Our horses are few, and diarrhea kills as many as bullets.

Thoughts of you are the only bright spots in my days.

Your loving,

Thomas Divers

May 11, 1864

My Dearest Susan,

We engage in a bloody game of cat and mouse, doing most of our fighting on horseback at Yellow Tavern.

Major General James Stuart, our commander, led us often into battle. Our enemy attempted to destroy railroad lines, steal our supplies, and threaten our capital! It is beyond my comprehension.

Stuart received his mortal wound, being shot in the stomach. I was one of the soldiers who rushed to assist him, with Homer by my side as always. I can still hear the General's last words, as he yelled for us to go back and do our duty.

Again, the writer Homer comes to mind: "…and what he greatly thought, he nobly dared."

With fondest regards,

Thomas Divers

May 18, 1864

My Dearest Susan,

Our country is shaken, but I believe in the sacredness of the cause for which we are battling.

Many men suffer with sickness, the most fatal being measles. I have been ill with dysentery and sent to a makeshift hospital in Ashland, Virginia. Still my loyal dog accompanies me.

Death and the devil have cast a gloom from which the South may never recover. We have much to fear in this ill-fated country.

Yours truly,

Thomas Divers

May 23, 1864

My Dearest Susan,

This makeshift hospital is a house near the railroad tracks. Men here wait desperately to hear from family, wives, and sweethearts. God bless the postmaster and all connected to the mail.

I am saddened to witness the despair of soldiers when their names are not called at post time, and I know my face shows the same. If I had but one letter from you—a ribbon or a clip of your hair—things might be more bearable. How I hold to the vision of your quivering lip and single tear.

Homer stays on the porch, waiting for me to come outside. The men find comfort in his presence, as do I. He does not seem to mind my deplorable condition. Would you?

The upper rooms are for surgeries and amputations. The cries of agony clutch at my heart and force me to cover my ears, but I have found a place in the cellar where I can get away from the screams and smells, so it is only you that my thoughts dwell upon.

Despite the horrors of war, I plan to live on if only to put this journal in your hands. Then you will know that my love for you is ever true.

So far, I have not contracted the "itch" called measles, but whelps and lice have grown as big as grains of wheat on my now-emaciated body.

I should not write of this to you, but I am thinking it does not matter. I, who always prided myself on cleanliness and a high moral character, have fallen low, having written such things to a woman such as you.

I send you all my love,

Thomas Divers

May 25, 1964

My Dearest Susan,

The doctors do their best, but there are so many of us now that the hospital overflows. Daily more wounded and ill arrive from the train. There is no place to put them.

If only you had seen fit to give me your love, your hand, your heart, I should have more of a will to live. Having little parchment left in my journal, or light to write by, I choose my words sparingly.

As always, my dog remains by my side.

Thomas Divers

May 27, 1964

My Dear Thomas,

It is spring but without you it isn't really. I cannot afford the luxury of one sweet thought of you, for it would tear me apart. But how can I not think of you when the dogwoods bloom and the butterflies appear? The world is lonely, and I am lost.

I received word that you were in the battle at Yellow Tavern and survived but are likely wounded. I pray this letter will find its way to you.

This past winter, my mother's struggle was over, and she left to be with our Lord and Savior. It is only Father and I now.

I wish I could have written to you, but the consequences caused me to refrain until this, perhaps my only letter. Father's controlling nature grows stronger with each passing day as he intercepts all correspondence.

Every night I pray you will not think less of me because I obey his dictates, for I see no other way while he lives.

I close this letter with a quote from Kahil Gibran, for truer words have never been spoken: "Ever has it been that love knows not its own depth until the hour of separation."

Linda Kay Simmons

You are always in my heart,

Susan

May 29, 1864

My Dearest Susan,

I am aflame with love. Imagine my surprise at receiving a letter from you. I have read it a hundred times and keep it close to my heart.

It saddens me to write that an epidemic has taken over. The doctors do not agree whether it is yellow fever or congestive fever, but it kills us just the same. Within four days, a living man can become a corpse, cut down in the blush of life.

I have instructed Homer to stay at this house and be with the others, as he comforts them so. I tell him to eat and stay strong and not to follow me into death.

The path through the trees and bushes is muddy and thin, weaving like a snake through the woods. Yet those who can carry bodies and dig graves perform their duties with heavy hearts. Many have been buried behind the house. I am afraid no one will know of the men who lie in these unmarked graves, although I have been assured their names have been recorded. Please remember mine.

Thomas Divers

June 9, 1864

Farewell, Susan,

I shall die soon. I place these writings and my carving of Homer in a safe place, hoping they shall be found.

I pray my bones and those of my fellow soldiers shall be resurrected and buried properly.

I send you all my love until we meet in heaven.

In the name of Jesus Christ, my Savior.

Lieut. Thomas Divers

* * *

I have endless questions while reading the journal. Susan's silence is hard to bear, and I feel such pity for Thomas. How could she not write to him? She could have found a way without her father knowing. I cannot begin to imagine being loved the way Susan was, and I envy her for that.

When Susan finally writes to Thomas, my heart fills with love and hope for the star-crossed lovers, and I cry at their tragic ending. I glance around. Did Thomas actually die in this very cellar? Was he buried in the woods behind my house, where I sometimes seek refuge from my life?

I read the journal several more times, inscribing it onto my heart, then I hide away in my bedroom. It's late and I need to sleep, although I doubt I will.

The next day, I return to the cellar. I place my hand between the gaping stones where I found the journal and grope further. My hand feels something small and smooth. Could it be? I pull the item out and carry it to the light for examination. Like the journal, it is wrapped in strips of fabric.

Carefully, I pull the rotten material away until a figurine of Homer lies in my palm, just as Thomas described him in the journal. A tingling starts in my hands and quickly travels through my whole body. Homer is Wolfdog!

What is happening? I ask the figurine.

You are on the right path at last, the figurine replies.

Before leaving the cellar, I read the journal twice more, crying harder each time I do. *Is there someone I need to share this journal with?* I ask the figurine.

Something—or someone—whispers to me to keep my discoveries a secret, at least for now.

CHAPTER FORTY-ONE

Cinderella

I was wrong. Golden Prince comes for me one more time while our parents are looking at Arabian horses.

Late at night, a torrential November downpour lashes the trees outside. I hear someone bump clumsily against my bedroom door.

"Who is it?" I ask.

"Golden Prince," he slurs. "Let me in."

Anger courses through me like a shot of heroin as he pounds against the locked door. "Let me in!"

"You aren't coming in here ever again," I shout. "I'm not a small defenseless girl anymore. I'm a grown woman of twenty-one!"

His rage seems to grow as he pummels the door. Harder, faster, then a barrage of kicking. "You can't tell me no!"

My flesh burns hot, and I feel parts of my body disappearing, trying to be invisible so he can't hurt me again. But those are the reactions of the old me. Wolfdog's senses sharpen, and the Confederate soldiers are by my side. Picking up my bedside lamp, I march to the door and open it wide, ready to attack.

As my eldest brother crosses the threshold, I crash the lamp down on his head. He falls like an acorn in a harsh wind. "I'll kill you if you ever touch me again, you son of a bitch." Bending down, I hold a sharp piece of broken lamp against the jugular vein of his throat.

Golden Prince rises to his feet and backs away while I hold on to my weapon, ready to do battle. He hurries down the stairs, his breathing labored. Then he opens the front door and disappears into the rain.

I listen as the leaves squelch beneath his cowardly feet as he makes his way to the shoddy Volkswagen bus and his miserable life. I am no longer afraid. On October 30, 1978, I have fought my attacker and won!

That night, as a golden arc of light shines on the walls and ceiling of my bedroom, two Confederate soldiers appear on either side of my bed. One morphs into an orb of pink light, and I hear a rich, comforting voice of indiscernible gender: *I am Haziel, angel of divine mercy and forgiveness.* The sound of the name leaves me with a feeling of peace beyond anything I can understand. *What's happening to me?*

One of the soldiers who stands before me is the same one who cradled me in my sleep so long ago. He steps forward and salutes. I take a deep breath, not knowing what might happen next. As he nods slightly, I notice his blue eyes and the heavy buttons on his wool coat. His hair is brown and wavy, his beard sparse and unruly.

"There is no need to be afraid," he whispers. "You've found my journal; I knew you would. Homer was with me in battle and came to this hospital to watch over me and the other soldiers. I willed him to stay here with you until we could all be together."

As he speaks, my bottom lip quivers, and a single tear rolls down my face. I know deep within that what he says is true! I want to run away and flee this house and my life in order to be with this soldier.

As I process my new awareness, he leans forward, close enough for me to pick up his appealing musky scent. His lips flutter across my cheek, and my breath becomes short and shallow. *This can't be happening, can it?* Then I hear his words in my mind, as plainly as if he is speaking them aloud: *Clear your soul of worries, my beautiful butterfly. This will work out in the end.*

How I want to believe him. How I need to believe him.

Then he pulls away from me, turns his face toward heaven, and disappears.

For hours I sit quietly, holding on to those precious moments.

It doesn't occur to me just how late I've slept, as my room stays dark with the shades down. When I glance at my clock, I see it's nearly one in the afternoon. A fresh wave of tears bursts from my eyes. Everything before the arrival of my soldier and the angel Haziel feels dirty and horrible.

At 1:30 p.m., I enter the living room, still wearing my pajamas. Mother stands at the coffee table scooping up handfuls of peppermint candies and putting them in her purse. She unwraps one and pops it into her mouth.

"Would you like one?" she asks.

"No, thank you."

"I have a list of chores for you to do today."

"Mother, it's the last day of November, and I'm taking the day off."

"A day off?" She laughs. "I never get a day off, plus you've slept through most of this one."

"Well, I'm taking one today."

"To do what, may I ask?"

"I'm going to take a walk and then do nothing at all."

I take a quick shower and dress, wondering if my soldier or Haziel are nearby. Could they still be in my room? Somewhere else in the house? Was it just hours ago that I had this experience?

I resolve to no longer go through my days as a sleepwalker, my body moving as if it weighs a thousand pounds. I need to find out what's happening to me.

Snowflakes descend from the sky and lightly cover the ground as I walk out the front door. Glancing about in search of my guardian angel, I ask, Which way would you have me to go? A warm feeling spreads through me, and I head toward the bookstore. Once inside, I know I've made the right decision.

The smell of cinnamon and fresh coffee fills the air, and a saleswoman greets me with a lovely smile. Everything about today is brighter. I flip through books and magazines while Wolfdog waits outside.

After I examine most of the limited books on angels, another title catches my attention: *The Sleeping Prophet* by Edgar Cayce. I don't know how long I read—ten minutes or two hours—but at closing time, I purchase the book and can't wait to read it from start to finish in bed tonight. I am fascinated by this man who writes of his remarkable prophecies and insights into the soul. Though Mr. Cayce doesn't say much about angels, I still want to learn more about them too, and I will. I'm on a mission.

As I exit the store, a squall of snow bursts from the sky, the flakes falling heavy on my head and shoulders, which is uncommon weather here for late November. There isn't a single soul scurrying along the slippery sidewalks as I make my way home.

* * *

For weeks I check out books from the library and research angels. Eventually, I even catch a city bus to Richmond, Virginia, and haunt the used bookstores there.

"I believe I have what you're looking for," says Herbert, the owner of a small musty bookstore on the outskirts of the city. He peers at me over his wire-rimmed spectacles. "This book was written years ago by a Jewish scholar of the Kabbalah. I cannot sell it to you, but you may study it at the table by the door."

Sitting down to read, I can barely breathe as I gingerly turn the pages of the eighty-year-old volume of esoteric knowledge. And then I find him—my angel is in the worn-out book!

Angel Haziel brings healing and freedom from the weight and misery of past mistakes, debts, and bonds. Haziel offers the gift of forgiveness and the honor of reconciliation with oneself, family, and the earth. When in need of grace, support, friendship, and altruism, Haziel may offer guidance to those in search of these gifts.

I wish there were more to read about Haziel, but the book is in poor condition with pages missing. Copying the words down in my notebook, I leave with a feeling of elation.

The burden of being me is lighter. For the first time, I laugh at myself, understanding something I haven't before: the power of love to nurture and heal.

When I walk into the house at 8:00 p.m., Father is sitting in his recliner wearing his bedroom slippers and a dirty blue velveteen bathrobe. His jaw hangs open, and there are pouches under his eyes. An open *Time* magazine is in his lap.

"Let me help you get into bed," I say, feeling Haziel's energy flow through me. "It's dark outside and still snowing."

"Let me smoke another cigarette and then we'll go." Father lights up, inhales, and coughs. After spitting phlegm into the slop jar at his feet, he gets up. Leaning on me, he shuffles to the bedroom and gets in his bed. I cover him up, then take out his dentures and set them on the table next to the Poligrip. The room smells of Vick's VapoRub.

"Mother's out?" I say, thinking of how much Father has aged recently.

"As usual," he says. "It's no fun for her being saddled with me."

I don't respond, knowing it is true. But I do broach another topic. "Father, do you believe in angels?"

"Never given it much thought. Maybe when I was a small boy, I did. Before I was taken."

"I'm sorry that happened to you," I say. "It wasn't right."

"You're a good girl. I want you to know that. Now it's time I close my eyes."

I nod and choke back a sob. I wish I could tell him he was a good father, but I can't lie.

"Good night," I say as I turn off the light and close the door.

I hope Father has an angel. I hope everybody does.

CHAPTER FORTY-TWO

Pissant

There are concrete gnomes and flowerpots full of pansies on our front porch. I don't know how they got there. Father walks with an old man's shuffle and continually coughs from the asbestos fibers embedded in his lungs. With perpetual hacking and fingers stained yellow, he stubs out one cigarette and immediately lights another. He does not talk to me. When I am around him, I feel as if a concrete gnome is weighing heavy on my chest.

The moon is full on June 19, 1977. When I go to Father's room to say good night, I find him lying facedown on the floor beside his La-Z-Boy recliner and an overflowing ashtray. It's 9:00 p.m., and no one is home but me. Not knowing what to do, I cover him with a blanket and wait for the others to return.

* * *

I feel grief and remorse at his death. But why did he call me—his own son—Pissant? Nothing hurt worse than that. When I press Cinderella for answers, she speaks of a conversation she had with him a few years before his death.

"No one was in the house but Father and I, when I got up my nerve and told Father you raped me. He shut me down, saying it was a private family affair, and I wasn't to tell Mother. He advised me to bury my bitterness, forgive you, and never speak of it again."

"What? He never mentioned it to me," I say, baffled. "Why do you think that was?"

"He didn't want to open a kettle of worms with Mother is my guess. It had already happened and there was no taking it back."

"But why didn't you tell him about Golden Prince? Our brother was the orchestrator of our crimes. I never would have touched you if it hadn't been for him. You ratted me out instead."

Cinderella frowns and looks regretful. "I didn't want to invoke Mother's wrath, given how much she reveres our brother, and who knows what Golden Prince would have done to me then? And you *did* molest me." She sighs. "I should have gone to the police to report him, but I didn't know that when I was little. Can you imagine how Mother would have reacted if Golden Prince had been convicted of rape and jailed? You could have been arrested too, by the way, and sent to juvie."

"I always thought Father hated me, and now I know that he must have. In his mind, I was the son who raped his baby girl. No wonder he called me Pissant."

"I'm sorry I didn't tell him about both of you," Cinderella says. "Not that it would have changed anything."

Father is dead at fifty-seven, and I'm twenty-five. I'm paralyzed and strangled by life, not knowing what to do next. I want Father to love and approve of me as he does Golden Prince, but now it's too late.

CHAPTER FORTY-THREE

Cinderella

Mother doesn't want to have a funeral, so she, my brother, and I circle Father's bed to say goodbye as we wait for the local funeral home owner and his men to come and take the body away for cremation. Golden Prince isn't here, and I'm glad. He's given Mother one of his usual lame excuses.

"You'll take good care of him?" Mother asks as Father is transferred to the funeral home's gurney.

"Yes, ma'am, with the utmost respect," the owner says.

We watch as they wheel away Father.

Mother's show of caring for Father touches me. I haven't witnessed it for some time.

A month later, on July 20, Mother, my brothers, and I gather to spread Father's ashes. It's a beautiful day in the mid-eighties, not a cloud in sight. Mother has brought a blanket, so she spreads it on the ground, along with a picnic basket containing Father's ashes, champagne, and glasses.

Champagne flutes in hand, we walk to the pasture where Chestnut and Lady Day are; they were Father's pride and joy. We each scatter a handful of ashes as the Arabians look on. Chestnut paws the ground, and Lady Day lets out a loud whinny, as if saying goodbye. Father would have loved the sight of them watching our impromptu ceremony.

"Your father had a hard start in life," Mother says. "But he loved all of us and worked hard to prove it. May he rest in peace."

"To Father," we say in unison as we raise our glasses and clink them.

Mother tries to look respectful in her new role of widow by wearing mostly black. But it doesn't take long before she has a new lease on life, having found hope through Walter Cronkite.

Mr. Cronkite has informed her via the television that Anna Manahan, the woman who claims to be Anastasia, has married an American professor and lives in Charlottesville, Virginia. He reports that they live as eccentrics in a sprawling home with cats, dogs, and bags of garbage. I laugh about the "eccentric" part—and the bags of garbage. Perhaps there's a connection between Mother and Anna Manahan after all.

According to the report, though, it cannot be officially determined that Anna Manahan is Anastasia; therefore, Anna cannot claim the remaining Romanov fortune. This news does not deter Mother in the least. Attempting to look like Russian royalty, she wears stoles, hats, and coats made from the hides of small murdered creatures. She tells anyone who will listen that her mother, Anna Manahan, lives only an hour away, and they will soon be united.

I tell her it's wrong to brag about something that may never happen and remind her of the letters she's written to Anna Manahan that were returned unopened.

I beg her not to wear dead animals. She doesn't listen.

CHAPTER FORTY-FOUR

Golden Prince

Mother doesn't want anyone knowing her business, especially the Department of Rehabilitation and Housing. Its August 1979, and Father's been dead for a couple of months. Since his demise, with a little snooping, I've learned a few of Mother's secrets, such as the source of the mysterious fire on Eton Lane that burned her double-mortgaged property to the ground. Without Father to do her bidding, she takes matters into her own hands. And so do I.

My chin is weak, so I've grown a Fu Manchu. I like my mustache and the two tendrils that extend past my jawline. I attempt to grow a third from my chin but with little success other than a few scraggly hairs. My new wire-rimmed glasses help with the appearance I'm trying to achieve: I want to look

Vietnamese.

I devour every word of *Rolling Stone*. The articles, artwork, and music are about personal freedom, and I'm all about that.

I hate it when Pissant comes around. I don't want anyone knowing he's my brother, and he's a real embarrassment. He has horrible body odor, and he's always saying something stupid about us as kids or telling some lame-ass joke, the same way Father did. Plus, he's into affirmations and goes around bestowing blessings on everyone. He's bought into the whole new-age thing.

"Take those affirmations off my bathroom mirror," I yell at him when he comes to the house.

"But you'll see them whenever you brush your teeth," he says. "They'll put positive thoughts in your mind. It says in Proverbs 23:7, 'As a man thinketh in his heart, so is he.'"

"I don't care what the Bible says! Take them down now, you weirdo!'

He's been out of sorts since Father died. He's been missing practices and gigs with the Swinging Kings and wants to hang with me and my roomies—partying and doing drugs—but it isn't going to happen.

"You can't come around here anymore," I tell him, "unless you call first. How can I make it with a girl if you show up uninvited?"

"But you never answer your phone," he says.

"My point exactly. Stay away."

My little brother leaves with a hangdog face. I don't care. I just want him to leave me the hell alone.

My preference is to rent rooms to single girls from the university. "I'm a Mensa, you know," I tell them, expecting admiration while I sit in a fog of marijuana smoke in my bedroom. None of them question why I didn't go on to college.

I spar and debate philosophy and world events with my young, dazed, stoned roommates and their friends. One day, Paracelsus, the medical pioneer and occult philosopher, appears to me in a haze of rainbows and waterfall. After that, I encourage my roommates to take psychedelic drugs.

"You can control your body processes," I tell one stoned blonde. "And I can help you do it." I fail to mention that I am horny, hot, and hungry from the hashish I've just smoked. "With the right drugs, a Hindu monk can walk over red-hot coals unharmed or place himself in a state of hibernation."

"And you can do this?" she says. "Walk on red-hot coals, I mean?"

"Sure. It's just mind over matter. I've done it many times."

My roommates seem to move out quickly but are always followed by new fresh-faced students who answer the ads I place in the college paper.

* * *

Sunlight filters through my bedroom window, and the temperature in my room tells me it's cold out. I roll over, pull the blankets and pillows all around me, and try to nod off. No use.

Opening my sleep-filled eyes to a splitting headache, I shuffle to the bathroom, brush my teeth, light a cigarette, pick yesterday's newspapers up off the floor, and sit on the toilet waiting for a dump. Speaking of dumps, it's hard to believe I've been living in this shithole for years.

When my mission is accomplished, I shower, dress, make coffee, and light a joint, blowing out any negative energy in a cloud of Mary Jane. Through the living room window, I watch the human hamsters scurry around in their mindless lives. I'm a free spirit, an adventurer, and I start my days serenely, knowing I am my own master.

I have a scale for weighing pot, a supply of small plastic bags, a decent stereo, a lava lamp by my bed, and a secondhand baby grand. Between the rents I collect, my dope sales, and what Mother pays me for collecting payments, I'm doing well.

Students from the university drop by constantly, wanting to get high. We listen to music and discuss the latest issue of *Rolling Stone* and the Vietnam war. If there's a hot chick around, I might get to screw her. Life doesn't get much better than this.

"They invited me to audition for the symphony orchestra, but I turned it down," I say to whomever drops by. "Too many rehearsals and not enough pay." It impresses people when I tell them this. The truth is, I wasn't asked because I didn't apply.

With the help of LSD and meditation, I connect with universal consciousness. Chanting channeled words with half-closed eyes, I give thanks to Timothy Leary and share my experiences with others.

Hallucinogens and cosmic signs reveal to me that I'm the grandson and reincarnation of Rasputin. It only makes sense. I'm a prophet with an enormous dick.

CHAPTER FORTY-FIVE

Anastasia

My daughter has just turned twenty-three. My first impression of Cinderella as a baby was the right one. She is an ugly duckling and my project gone wrong.

"You should wear lipstick," I tell her. "You're pale. If you exercise and lose fifty more pounds, you'll have a splendid figure and could find a boyfriend."

She thinks I don't notice the mascara streaking down her tear-stained cheeks when I tell her these things, but my sympathy will only make her weaker. She needs to buck up and take my suggestions to heart.

She cooks and cleans not only at home but at my other properties after tenants move out. There's never been a question of her leaving my house and getting a job of her own. Where would she go? What would she do? I wonder what Betty Friedan would think of her. A lost cause, probably.

Despite her sessions with that odd Moon Woman, Cinderella does what I tell her, but she's occasionally defiant. Moon Woman has cast a spell over my daughter, and I don't like it.

My middle child—Pissant, they call him, though I don't know why—is like a stranger to me. At twenty-six, he still plays with the Swinging Kings but doesn't earn enough to live on. He's so unlike his father and me, with little to no ambition.

He rents a basement room from some man named George. At least it has an outside entrance. I know the street and its dilapidated houses well, so I can only imagine what a basement apartment must be like.

It's better this way, though. I could never trust Pissant to help me with repairs or payment collections. He's clumsy and too much of a bleeding heart, and I'll never forget the day he fell off of the roof. Plus, he drinks like a sailor. I smell it on him when he comes around. He's probably smoking dope too; I'm no dummy. It's better that Pissant lives in his hovel than with me.

Linda Kay Simmons

At least one of my children is doing well. Ah, Golden Prince, my shining star.

CHAPTER FORTY-SIX

Golden Prince

The songs of the '70s are downers and the new '80s music isn't much better. I particularly hate "Bridge Over Troubled Water" by Simon and Garfunkel, and I try not to heave when the Carpenters' "(They Long to Be) Close to You" comes on the radio.

It's March 12, 1981, and the snow is deep. I'm curled up with *Rolling Stone*. I can't get enough of the provocative photography or the poems by Richard Brautigan and Allen Ginsberg.

Later in the day, I trip while listening to Jagger. I'm convinced he's the reincarnated Oscar Wilde, and the idea makes me laugh hysterically.

While still high, I watch *The Picture of Dorian Gray*. I figure it out, of course, because that's who I am. I need someone to do a painting of me. Better still, I'll create a self-portrait tomorrow.

CHAPTER FORTY-SEVEN

Anastasia

I'm heartbroken. They report on the evening news that Anna Manahan died of pneumonia today, February 12, 1984.

Walter Cronkite calls her an imposter who claimed to be Grand Duchess Anastasia of Russia. I shall never forgive Walter. After all, there is no actual proof either way.

But in my heart, I know the truth: she is my mother. It has to have been Anna's husband, John, who kept her away from me.

CHAPTER FORTY-EIGHT

Pissant

I'm driving my blue Thunderbird home after a night of band practice, drinking and smoking pot. Blinded by another's high beams, I become disoriented, see a deer in front of me, swerve to miss it, and career off the road. The car rolls, and I can't get out.

In the hospital, I hear strangers' voices talking about me. I can't make them understand that I hear them, and my eyes won't open.

"The patient, a white male, age thirty-two, suffered severe head trauma. He has brain swelling and a broken right tibia. He's had a prior concussion. We need to get him into surgery now."

A week later, I regain consciousness, but no one is there. I ask for Mother, and a kind nurse calls her. Mother shows up hours later.

"Hello, sleepyhead," Mother says. "It's time you came around."

"I don't understand what's going on," I moan. "Was I hurt? The doctors haven't told me anything."

"You were in a car wreck and the airbags didn't deploy. They put sutures throughout your scalp and above your left eye. And the doctors installed a steel plate in your right leg. You're fortunate to be alive."

For months after the accident, I'm in physical agony. Drinking and smoking help blur the pain, but living in George's damp, smelly, cold basement doesn't help. Despite the steel plate, I pace the floors, unable to control my impulse to walk. Then I notice something in a matchbook cover I pick up at the corner market while buying cigarettes. It's an ad for the Universal Life Church. I immediately write for information, although I can barely scrawl my name with the nerve damage in my right arm and hand.

"I can get a Doctor of Divinity degree from the ULC for twenty dollars," I tell my brother from a pay phone. "The church has already ordained over a million ministers. Do you know anything about it?"

"There was a rumor that claimed ordination from the ULC would qualify for a draft exemption for religious reasons," Golden Prince says. "I know people who got it for that reason, only to find out it wasn't true. But a few of them took the religious part seriously and now they have small congregations, mostly the hippie kind. They perform ceremonies, I think."

"Why didn't you tell me about it?"

"What was the point? It couldn't keep me out of the draft. And how was I supposed to know you'd turn into a religious freak after seeing *Jesus Christ Superstar*?"

"The ULC has only one belief—that it's every person's right to interpret what is right," I say. "They accept people of all religions. It sounds like what I've been looking for."

"Good luck with it, little brother. I guess everyone needs a dream. But me, personally, I'd rather smoke dope and get laid."

"Did you know they believe in reincarnation? I think that's pretty cool. They respect the individual options of their members. Maybe I had to be in the wreck to understand all this. Maybe it's a sign."

"Ha! Now you can be Reverend Pissant," he says, laughing. "Let me know when your ordination comes through and we'll celebrate."

CHAPTER FORTY-NINE

Cinderella

I fill my wine glass at the kitchen counter, trying to remember today's date. I glance at the front of the evening newspaper on the table. Sitting down to take a needed break, I see that it's Saturday, March 14, 1987. When I flip to the horoscopes, I realize we're under the sign of Pisces. Sidney Sheldon's book, *Windmills of the Gods*, is on the bestseller list, Ronald Reagan is still our Republican president, and Margaret Thatcher is the UK Prime Minister. Nothing has changed.

The sink is full with two days' worth of dirty dishes. I'll probably have the entire bottle of wine finished before I can clean up this mess. A long sigh escapes my lips as I notice the mouse droppings on the floor. I'm so tired that I toy with the idea of going to bed early, but Mother calls out. Her words sound garbled and strange. Just thirty minutes ago, she was finishing up paperwork on the dining room table.

The years haven't been kind to her. At sixty-five, she wears a crooked wig of garish red to hide her almost nonexistent hair. She no longer bathes, but sprays Tigress Perfume on herself several times a day. Thick, clunky diamond rings adorn her age-spotted fingers, and her creaky voice gives orders from sneering lips.

"What is it, Mother?" I say, entering the dining room. Then I notice how badly her hands are shaking, and she seems unable to answer me.

I call an ambulance, ride in it with her to the hospital, and then wait. After several hours, a nurse calls me into Mother's room, where a doctor has finished examining her.

"Your mother is stable now, but she suffered an ischemic stroke. For a short duration, her brain received inadequate blood, causing damage, although it's hard to say how much. We're treating her with medication."

"Is the damage permanent?"

"Time will tell, but I expect she'll improve. I don't know how much, though."

"Mother has a fighting spirit," I say. This doctor doesn't know Mother or her cast-iron will.

I call Golden Prince, even though it's one in the morning, to give him the doctor's report. After the sixth ring, he answers with a groggy voice.

"A blood vessel burst," I gush out. "It's left Mother with muscle weakness on her left side, blurred vision, and sensitivity to light. To help with the double vision, the doctor put a patch over her right eye."

"Mother as a pirate," he says, chuckling. "Somehow it fits."

"Are you coming to the hospital?"

"There's no need if you're there."

"That fine," I say, not wanting to see him either. "We need to let our brother know. Can you at least do that?"

"I'll try tomorrow, but there's no telling where he is. Probably standing on a street corner with his Bible, trying to convert the whores. I have to go." He hangs up.

* * *

Mother's strength improves quickly, although her mobility and balance are not the same. She needs a cane.

Six weeks after the stroke, she is back in the game, sipping cheap champagne as her magnified eyes swim behind the thick lenses in her glasses.

She still does the books but is more dependent on me than ever. I drive her to the bank in her station wagon, with frequent stops at her lawyer's office. Peeking at the papers one day, I notice the beneficiary line is blank. It makes sense, since Father is dead. I don't give it further thought.

Since Mother's stroke, Golden Prince still claims he can't find our brother. I haven't seen Pissant in over three months, but he shouldn't be this hard to find. I look in Mother's address book and find an address for him on Elm Avenue, with a note saying he lives in the house's basement. I don't want to worry Mother with this, but it's odd she hasn't asked to see him. Maybe it's a side effect of the stroke?

Driving Mother's station wagon on June 12, I get out of the car, walk around the old frame house, and knock on the basement door.

Pissant answers with a blanket wrapped around his shoulders, despite the warm temperature. He looks at my face and must notice my confusion. "I stay chilled," he says. "Since the accident."

Stepping inside, I look around. There's no bathroom or indoor plumbing. Only a cot, a chair with the stuffing falling out, a wooden table, a hotplate, and a lamp, plus a messy pile of clothes on the floor near his trombone.

"How can you live like this?" I say. "Come home. You can have a bathroom and a proper kitchen."

My brother laughs. "Mother wants too much rent."

"What do you mean?"

"She doesn't think I can do maintenance as well as Father, and Golden Prince says I only get in his way when he tries to get things done. Mother says I have to earn my keep, and since she has no work for me, I'd have to pay room and board."

"I'm worried about you," I say, horrified by his disclosure. "I've got some cash in the station wagon. Why don't we at least go get something to eat?"

"I'm not one to turn down a free meal. Let's go."

I drive to Joe's Diner, a place he used to love. I watch as he downs two burgers, a double order of fries, and a shake. The last time I saw him, he was on a vegetarian diet.

"I'm no shrink," I say, "but do you think it would help if you talk to a therapist about what's going on? I have someone I talk to, and I attend meditation classes. It helps."

"Yeah, I tried once. I talked to a psychologist who takes on free patients at the clinic. Told him I was raped as a kid, but I didn't get into details of how many times. All he did was refer me to a doctor who gives me free pain meds because of the wreck."

"What else did the psychologist say?"

"He said now that I'm an adult, I need to confront my rapist if he's still alive, and if not, we could work on it in his office through role-playing. I've thought of reporting him to the police, but I don't have any proof and it's been a long time."

"Are you going confront him?"

"I've seen Choirmaster in his front yard working in his flower beds. I've thought about stopping, but I can't get up the nerve."

"I'll go with you if you want. Because of what he and the other men did to you, it affected my life too."

"There's no use in it. Right now, I'm a fucked-up mess, and George has told me to move out." He reaches into his pocket, takes out a bottle, and swallows a handful of pills. "I don't have last month's rent or this month's either, and Golden Prince doesn't want me coming around anymore, much less asking for money."

"Why would you want to see him? He ruined both our lives."

"Hey, little sister, don't forget I'm an ordained minister with the Universal Life Church. God has a plan for me. I'll get through this. Don't worry about me."

After we finish eating, I drop my brother back off at George's house. I don't feel good about any of this. He's in pain physically and emotionally, and I feel powerless to help.

CHAPTER FIFTY

Golden Prince

Waking up in a cold sweat, I glance at the bedside clock: 6:00 a.m. Having thrashed about all night and able to sleep only minutes at a time, I keep seeing images of Mother in my brain.

Mother has become a drooling mass of flesh holding court at her dining room table, and she's lost her edge. Since her stroke, I haven't done repairs to her slummy real estate, but she doesn't know that. It's hard for her to get around on her walker, and she believes whatever I tell her.

I swing my legs over the side of the bed and shuffle to the kitchen to make a pot of coffee. After lighting a cigarette, I retrieve the morning paper from the stoop. Today is Easter Sunday, April 19, 1987. Pouring a cup of java, I sit down to read the paper, but it's too hard to concentrate.

I've converted all of Mother's real estate into rental properties. It's easier than trying to find buyers for the houses and then financing the places. Plus, there are too many inspections and regulations. Rentals have little of that garbage. But now some houses sit empty, and the city has condemned several properties. I've kept that from Mother, of course, by collecting the mail and changing her phone number to "unlisted." Soon the coffer will be dry, and whatever's left I don't plan on sharing with Pissant and Cinderella.

Now that Pissant lives on the streets, he's no longer a problem. I can handle him. A born-again preacher—who could have thought that up? Like any respectable homeless guy, he always has a bottle of Ripple in his back pocket, paid for by his panhandling.

I didn't tell my sister that I'd recently seen Pissant in a decrepit area of downtown, his face pale, his eyes vacant and confused. I was close enough to see that his clothes were unwashed and that a green rubber band—the kind that goes around newspapers—held back his hair. He didn't notice me, so I walked on.

Cinderella takes it upon herself to arrange a visit with a

neurologist for my little brother. Turns out he's got brain damage—no surprise there. But the doctor also tells Cinderella that he shows signs of Alzheimer's disease. I thought that was something only old people got, but not in Pissant's case, I guess.

Cinderella, however, is a different story. She stays busy cooking, cleaning, and changing Anastasia's shit-filled pants. She's resentful of me and spits out hatred with great precision and highfalutin words.

Just yesterday she scolded me with the usual diatribe when I went by the house to sort through Mother's mail. "If you'd help Mother more," she said, "I could go to classes and workshops like you do."

"But you have your charlatan, Moon Woman, although she doesn't seem to do you much good," I said while smoking a cigarette.

She gave me a wicked glare. She doesn't like me talking about Moon Woman, but I'm not about to spend more time with Mother than I absolutely have to.

I stub out my cigarette, knowing I drug, drink, and smoke too much, but I don't really care.

CHAPTER FIFTY-ONE

Cinderella

It's July 18, 1987, a date that's now emblazoned in my memory. The hot and muggy afternoon weighs upon me, but I plan to visit the stables for a ride when it cools down. Luke's reputation as a skilled horseman has grown, and he's bought the stables along with additional acreage. Some evenings, he mounts his horse and rides alongside Chestnut and me. Usually we don't talk; there is no need.

When Luke calls me that afternoon with fear in his voice, I'm surprised. "Chestnut has fallen," he says, "and her leg is swollen, possibly broken. She needs you with her."

I grab my purse and the keys to Mother's station wagon, then leave the house in a panic. I'm too nervous to drive, but I need to get to Chestnut as quickly as possible. My hands perspire as I clutch the steering wheel. *Please God, listen to me this one time and let Chestnut be all right.*

As soon as I arrive, Luke drives me in his truck to the field where he found Chestnut. Luke's face is lined with worry. "She's in a great deal of pain," he says, "but the vet is on his way. Smellin' your scent and hearin' your voice will comfort her."

My heart breaks when I see Chestnut lying on the ground in distress, and I can't hold back tears. When she sees me, she raises her head and softly nickers. Paul Lane, the vet, arrives within minutes and starts his examination.

Soon he shakes his head and turns to me. "Looks to me like maybe Chestnut was kicked in the second metacarpal bone, causing it to shatter."

Now it's Luke's turn to shake his head. He turns to me. "Your mother's mare doesn't get along with the other horses. I shouldn't have turned Lady Day and Chestnut out together. I'm so sorry. I made a huge mistake."

A lump forms in my throat when I see the sadness in Luke's eyes.

"You can't be sure how this happened," the vet says to Luke. "Sometimes horseplay escalates to rough play."

"What can you do for her?" I ask. "She's young yet, only twelve."

"I'm afraid bone isn't possible to repair, at least not successfully."

I can't bear to see Chestnut suffer. Even with all the pain and abuse I've suffered in my life, none of it compares to the moment that I tell the vet to put Chestnut down with a lethal injection. I cradle her head in my lap as a peaceful death lays claim to her.

As she surrenders, a coyote comes out into the pasture, and an owl screeches. They are welcoming her spirit, I know. And Wolfdog is by my side.

Now Chestnut lives in my heart. She was a great teacher for me. She never judged, instead accepting me as I was. Horses don't lie.

CHAPTER FIFTY-TWO

Golden Prince

Waking to the sound of heavy rain, I stumble into the shower, dry off, and put on my favorite old jeans and a tattered, faded flannel shirt. My back hurts from sleeping on the pullout sofa after I fell asleep watching *The Twilight Zone*. I sit on the john for thirty minutes, reading an old issue of *Rolling Stone*. My bowels always give me trouble, even though I force myself to eat Grape Nuts every night before bed. They don't help.

When I finish with a less-than-impressive plop, I go to the kitchen and scramble eggs, covering them with tabasco sauce. I drink yesterday's coffee.

After eating, I light my bong and take a long toke of hashish. I'm so tired of taking Mother to the hospital for blood tests and meeting with doctors to discuss her recently diagnosed colon cancer. Hell, it's 1988, and I've been dealing with Mother since I was a kid. She's nothing but an inconvenience who interferes with my poetry readings and Buddhist practices. If only I could take over her business, my life would be perfect, assuming my siblings were out of the way too.

At thirty-eight, I'm tired of this shit. I hate my mother's putrid smell and slack-jawed mouth. Why doesn't she die? But I have a plan. I'll move her into a nursing home—but no, not really. I'll only pretend to.

Several hours later, I get in the old VW and drive to Mother's. I enter the horrible house, with its dirty dishes and foul smells. My sister, not as unwashed or obese as she used to be, helps me load Mother onto her wheelchair. Although Cinderella looks better these days, no one would want her, especially not me.

With considerable effort, I use a small metal ramp to wheel Mother into the back of the bus. I leave the rear door unlatched, and I cut the radio up to maximum volume. After backing out of the driveway and giving a farewell wave to Cinderella, I head straight to the freeway, where I slam on the brakes over and over. The wheelchair hits the back of the van repeatedly, and I chuckle each time Mother lets out a high-pitched scream.

I drive as fast as I dare, taking curves and swerving unnecessarily as I think about the high cost of nursing homes. But Mother doesn't fly out as planned. At least not yet. I've even practiced exactly what I'll say to the police officers: *My beloved mother... a horrible accident... so sad.*

CHAPTER FIFTY-THREE

Anastasia

I hunch over the table, using a magnifying glass as I review the bills. Writing checks with my sprawling scrawl, I add stamps, shuffle to the front porch on my walker, and place the bills in the outbox. Every day, my tasks get harder to manage. Colon cancer. But at least I can be grateful that Golden Prince takes care of me and his siblings.

There is something different about Cinderella these days. Her hair and clothes are clean, and she's lost weight, but I worry about her attending those Indian sweat lodges and meditation classes. People are putting strange ideas in her head, and just yesterday she told me to call her Susan!

Several times a day, the phone rings for her. *She has friends?* I don't know what's come over her. It's strange. Good thing I did what I did, giving Golden Prince power-of-attorney and making him executor of my estate. He'll watch over Cinderella and Pissant for me.

At 6:30 p.m., I turn on the news and find it hard to comprehend what Walter Cronkite says at first. He claims fate has taken a turn and that the remains of the Romanov daughters have been found in a mass grave. Anna's DNA has been compared to that of the remaining members of the British Romanovs, and it's been confirmed that she is not a Romanov.

My entire life is a lie. I scoop up my fanciest champagne glass, a bottle of André, and some Valium, and I climb into bed.

I die that night. I am sixty-nine.

And that's the way it is on October 17, 1991.

CHAPTER FIFTY-FOUR

Cinderella

It's December 23, 1991, and the lawyer's office is decorated with fake greenery and pinecones. The secretary shows me into an office with a metal table, two chairs on either side, and a battered wooden desk that overpowers the room. I expected more, but Mother always went for cheap, so I shouldn't be surprised that she hired the least expensive attorney she could find.

I never looked into Mother's financial records, which I know are a mess. I probably should have, but her papers always overflowed from multiple laundry baskets piled high on the dining room floor, where they sat for years.

The lawyer's hands are square with powerful fingers. He wears a gold pinky ring accented with a center diamond. I pick up the document he offers me and grasp it with both hands. There's a knock on the office door, and the lawyer lets Golden Prince in before returning to his swivel chair.

Golden Prince sits across from me and gives me a smug look.

"I knew your mother well," the lawyer says as he pastes on a fake smile and pushes a file toward me, "and this is what she wanted."

I take a few minutes to study what he's given me, then look up at him for clarification.

"As you can tell by the paperwork, Anastasia left her properties and the primary residence to her firstborn." He turns to me. "You, however, may live in the family home for the rest of your life and are to be given a monthly stipend as long as you assist your brother with the family business."

I sigh and shake my head. "I shouldn't have expected anything for myself—I know how she was—but she doesn't even mention my other brother. This can't be right; she must have left him something. Maybe one of the rental houses to get him off the streets?"

"She's depending on you and Golden Prince to look after him," the lawyer says. "With his afflictions, he can't be expected to handle money and could easily be taken advantage of. I thought you knew. She and Golden Prince came in just before her death and worked out what they thought was the best solution."

"This seems like neglect or something worse," I say, looking at the lawyer while purposely avoiding Golden Prince, although my words are meant for his ears. "Our brother could die from the cold or illness. He's had pneumonia and has been to the emergency room more than once. Do you know he sleeps in an abandoned car in the woods and has been attacked by bum bashers twice?"

"I'm hearing this for the first time," the lawyer says. "Your mother didn't share those details."

"It's true. There's a woman, Patricia, who works at the mission. She calls me when she sees or hears something alarming. She really cares about him. Just yesterday she suggested I call Social Services again to see if they can get him into public housing."

"Pissant goes to the mission for meals and to get out of the cold," Golden Prince says. "It's his choice to live on the streets."

"Even though it's you who helped put him there?"

The lawyer coughs to get our attention. "Let's get back to the matter at hand. It's up to Golden Prince to do what he sees fit regarding his brother."

Golden Prince nods in agreement. "There was no point in bothering you with any of this, Cinderella, because Mother put me in charge. You'll just have to trust me."

I laugh and can't stop. Tears stream down my face.

"There's something more," the lawyer continues after I compose myself. "At our last meeting, your mother told me her properties have second mortgages and are underwater. Interest rates being what they are, and with the ages of the properties, I'd advise they be sold as quickly as possible. Of course, you'll want to talk to a CPA, as I shouldn't be giving you financial advice, but you might as well know that her properties have been losing money for years."

"What about the mortgage payments that went to Mother?" I ask. "There are several of those properties."

My brother's lower lip droops as he sneers at me. "You've never had a head for business. I turned those houses into rental properties over the past several years." He shrugs. "There was no point in telling you."

"I bet Mother never knew that."

"Next time, you'd better have Moon Woman reshuffle her tarot cards," he says. "If she had, maybe things would have come out more in your favor."

I am about to speak when I feel Haziel's loving presence surround me, so instead I smile at my brother and feel pity for him. Little does he—or anyone—know that at that moment he already has Parkinson's disease.

A week later I get a call from Patricia. "Your brother has been taken away by ambulance. You need to get to Mercy Hospital as quickly as you can. He's had a severe heart attack."

I get there in time, but barely. I take my brother's large hand in mine, as he lies in a narrow bed hooked to wires and monitors. My mind flashes to another time when we were children pulling our rickety old wagon home together from Ferrell's Market. He placed his hand over mine then, wanting me to be safe. Now it's my turn.

"Glad you came," he said weakly. "I have little time."

"Is there anything I can do?"

"Yes, take my Bible," he whispers as I lean my ear close to his mouth. His breath is sour, but I don't care. In fact, I know already that I will miss it. "I want you to have it. There's a letter in it for you to mail. And please, tell me again that you forgive me."

My eyes fill with tears as I squeeze his hand. "Not only do I forgive you, but I love you. Very much." He does not open his eyes again.

My brother dies an hour later. It's a peaceful death, unlike his life.

That night, with a lit candle and a glass of red wine nearby, I open his Bible and find the letter—more of a note, really—which is not sealed. It's addressed simply to Choirmaster.

> *I want you to know you didn't ruin my life. I've forgiven myself for the sins I committed, and I have found joy doing what I was born to do, preaching the word. I've prayed for the darkness in your soul to be removed and will continue to do so from the other side. – Luther*

I mail the letter from my brother, Luther, to the man who sinned against him.

Because I have no money to bury my brother, Patricia arranges for him to be buried at Potter's Field. We are the only two people there when he is laid to rest, but somehow the moment feels full and complete. It's January 15 and fairly frigid outside, so we're bundled up in coats, scarves, and gloves. Patricia recites the Lord's Prayer over my brother and together we sing his favorite song, "Amazing Grace." Then we link arms and head to a nearby restaurant for hot chocolate.

After we warm up with a few sips of our beverages, Patricia tells me something interesting. "Did you know that the idea of Potter's Field began when Judas gave thirty pieces of silver to the Chief Priest and confessed, 'I have sinned in betraying innocent blood'? Upon consulting, the priests bought a potter's field as a burial site for strangers. It's in Matthew 27:3-27."

"Judas again," I mutter with a smile. "I should have known." My brother's life was a puzzle, and now all the pieces fit.

CHAPTER FIFTY-FIVE

Cinderella

My temporary cure is and always will be the rising of the sun.
Today is a new beginning, and I feel better than I have in a long
while. It's April 2, 1992, and I'm headed to Lexington in search
of Susan Meador's family. Moon Woman accompanies me and
does the driving.

As I gaze out the window lost in thought, Moon Woman speaks.
"Many people believe in fear more than they believe in love.
One day this won't be true for you."

"I hope you're right."

"I know I am." She reaches over and pats my hand.

"I think our first stop should be the library at Virginia Military

Institute," I say. "The letters I found spoke of Susan's father wanting to be the president of the college, and since he was a professor, I bet we find something."

After we arrive, I climb the steps of the formidable library with inexplicable trepidation, Moon Woman by my side.

The librarian, a kind-eyed, middle-aged woman, proves helpful. "The address you're looking for is near Stonewall Jackson's home, which you can tour if you'd like."

"We're more interested in talking with the ancestors of Susan Meador," I say. "Do you know if any of them live in the house now?"

"The house never left the original family's hands," the librarian says. "A great-granddaughter lives there. She's a delightful woman and comes to historical events from time to time with her husband and young daughter."

Spring in Virginia means flowering dogwoods, which enjoy a long and beautiful blooming season. I love the cherry dogwoods, which bloom in March, and the flourishing beauty of the pagoda dogwoods from May to June, but I'm not prepared for the majesty of the trees at 14 Washington Street. For a moment, it takes my breath away.

As Moon Woman parks the car, I'm overwhelmed with a sense of familiarity. The brick-and-stone, two-story dwelling is one I know well, although I'm certain I've never been here before. We exit the car and gaze at the home.

"Are you ready for this?" Moon Woman asks.

"If you don't mind, I'd like to stand here and take it all in."

"Breathe deeply, then we can walk up and knock when you're ready." She places a warm hand on my shoulder, then steps away to wait while I absorb the surroundings.

Thoughts of Thomas Divers swirl through my mind. *Is he with me now?* Above the large oak door, a pink and green orb of light glows. I can tell by Moon Woman's face that she sees it as well. I am on the precipice of the unexplainable. Together we approach the door, and I raise my hand and knock.

An attractive woman in her early thirties answers. "If you're looking for Stonewall Jackson's house, it's right over there," she says, pointing to it.

"No, it's this house we're looking for," I say. "Do you have a minute to speak with us? It's about Susan Meador and Thomas Divers."

Curiosity shines in her eyes. "Susan Meador is my great-grandmother, and I'm Amy. Why don't you come in? We can talk in the parlor."

Moon Woman and I glance hopefully at each other, then follow Amy in. The parlor is warm and inviting, even though the heavy wooden furniture and brocade drapes are from another era. School pictures are grouped together, storybooks lie open on the sofa, and an empty pizza box sits in the corner, not far from a pile of toys. It all suggests a house brimming with life.

"Excuse the mess," Amy says. "Have a seat where you like, but you might have to move a stuffed animal or two."

I like Amy immediately.

"We have so much family history in this house," Amy says, "and are incredibly fortunate; so many families lost everything in the war."

We make polite conversation before I get up the nerve to tell her about Thomas's letters, but I finally do. Sharing them feels like giving a part of myself away.

Amy listens attentively as I share my tale. She gasps at times and looks sad at others. "What you've told me sheds so much light on my great-grandmother. I'm so thankful you came to me."

"I've made copies of the letters," I say. "Would you like to have them?"

"Nothing would make me happier." She smiles, her eyes conveying immense gratitude.

I pull the pages from my purse and hand them to her. She immediately starts to read.

"This is unbelievable," she says when she finishes. "I want to share something with you now. The family Bible is in the library along with several portraits that might interest you. We've attempted to keep the library as close to the original as possible, for historical reasons, of course."

Moon Woman and I follow her into a large room lined with shelves of old books. An enormous wooden desk sits in the center, its front facing two straight-back chairs, while a stone fireplace anchors the rear wall. She retrieves a large King James Bible from a shelf, places it on the desk, then opens it to the family history section.

"As you can see here," she says, pointing to a particular handwritten entry, "Susan's father, Charles Meador, died a few years after the war. Susan was left alone in this big house and eventually married a close friend of her father's, Henry Burnett, who was quite a bit older than she. They had one child, my great-grandmother, before Henry died." She pauses, then gazes gently into my eyes. "There's one more letter, you know, but it was never mailed."

The news should surprise me, but somehow it doesn't, almost as if I already knew it existed.

Amy continues. "Because of that letter, which Susan wrote but never mailed to her Confederate soldier, I've often thought of what a tragic life she had. Would you like to read it?"

I nod enthusiastically, and Amy hands me the letter. I hold it in my trembling hand, open it, and read. In my wildest imagination, I never thought a moment like this could happen. I read:

Dearest Thomas,

I have received word that you no longer live, but forever you shall dwell in my heart.

For every year that passes, I shall plant a dogwood tree in your memory, for they were blooming when we said our goodbyes.

How I wish things could have been different, and we had

married. I wanted nothing more than to be your wife.

Yours forever,

Susan

When I finish reading, my heart fills with pain, as if someone has stabbed my soul, but the feeling passes quickly. I look up at Amy, gather myself, and manage to thank her. Then I hand the letter to Moon Woman.

"Feel free to look around the room," Amy offers. "I'll make tea and sandwiches for us. Also, over the fireplace is a portrait of Susan."

"Please don't go to all that trouble," I say. "I so appreciate your letting us into your lovely home."

"It's my pleasure. I'm often alone during the day, when my little girl is in school, so I welcome the company." She gazed at me for a moment. "You know, it's funny, but you look an awful lot like my great-grandmother." She points to the portrait. "Kind of strange, really."

When she leaves the room, Moon Woman and I walk toward the fireplace to take a closer look.

"There is an uncanny resemblance," Moon Woman says,

216

glancing between the portrait and me.

"Do you think it is me?" I whisper.

"Yes, I do."

CHAPTER FIFTY-SIX

Susan

I pass through the cemetery gates, then slow my pace as I traverse the familiar desolate path and light filters through the canopy of leaves above. I'm always impressed by the holly trees, rolling hills, and winding paths that overlook the James River. But more than that, Richmond's Hollywood Cemetery, where I am now, is a place of comfort and familiarity.

The groundskeeper shuffles past me. We are the only ones here at this early hour. When I'm absent from here, I long for the shady drive that meanders under the maples, the rosy glow before nightfall, and the angelic statues in their flowing stone garments, who look up beseechingly at God. Old men often fill the benches and absorb the ample sunshine, while the dead indulgently support them from above and below.

In 1869, a ninety-foot-tall granite pyramid was erected on the grounds as a memorial to the eighteen thousand enlisted men of the Confederate army and the twenty-eight Confederate generals who are buried here. Standing beside it, I feel small and unworthy of what I am about to attempt, which involves facing my eldest brother.

I have spearheaded the effort to contact the Richmond and Ashland Historical Societies by letter and phone. It is important they know of the soldiers buried behind the house where I grew up. It's hard for me to hand over the register of names and regiments that I found years ago, but I do. I want the men—particularly Thomas Divers—respectfully exhumed and laid to rest.

I've given Thomas's original journal and the carving of Homer to the Richmond Historical Society, although it's hard for me to part with the items. But a copy of Thomas's papers and Susan's letters are tucked into the Meador Bible, where they deserve to be.

Golden Prince has been uncooperative throughout the entire project. So now I stand on his front porch, rehearsing what I will say to him. He is playing the piano, and after I put my fist to the door, the music stops. After a short while, he opens the door and stares at me.

"I need to talk to you," I say.

He stands aside and gestures for me to enter. Once I'm in, I waste no time in stating my case.

He tells me it will cost big bucks, but for the right amount of money he'll sell the house to the city of Richmond and the property that extends through the woods. There is no use in negotiating with him further. The amount of money he wants is beyond ridiculous, so I take the matter into my own hands.

I go to the local paper and television stations. Correspondents and journalists subsequently report on his unwillingness to cooperate with the project. It becomes big news because the people of Virginia, particularly the residents of Ashland, feel strongly that the Confederate soldiers should be exhumed and buried properly.

Embarrassed by news articles and television broadcasts, Golden Prince offers me three thousand dollars to get the press off his back and paint him in a favorable light. He cannot take the hounding. I take the money but only after he accepts an offer from the State of Virginia for the house and property; it's far less than what he wants. I have one more term by which he must abide: He will pay for a granite tombstone I've picked out. It's to be placed in Potter's Field, with Luther's full name and "Gone But Not Forgotten" etched into the stone.

Once the sale is finalized, Moon Woman invites me to live with her, and I accept the offer, hoping that I've wiped my hands clean of Golden Prince forever.

Using metal detectors, historical archaeologists unearth two well-preserved skeletons, both of which wear faded, decomposed Confederate uniforms with small buttons. The discovery is unsettling, and I wonder if I'm looking at Thomas. Over a three-month period, the corpses of thirty-nine Confederate soldiers are found.

Once the bodies are exhumed, the city of Ashland condemns the house. Even though it's historic, the cost of restoring it proves prohibitive.

The Virginia Department of Historic Records documents the findings and concludes that most of the soldiers died from smallpox. Finally, the dead and the descendants who searched for them have closure.

Over the course of the next year, the City turns the property into a park with swing sets and jungle gyms. I smile whenever I drive by and see children playing. Where the house once stood, glossy-leafed rhododendron and mountain laurel bloom.

Thomas's bones, along with those of the other soldiers, gain placement in a crypt behind the granite pyramid. The soldiers have been honored, their names accounted for, and they are safely guarded by a bronze statue of Homer at the entrance to their place of rest.

CHAPTER FIFTY-SEVEN

Golden Prince

On June 19, 1992, I park my still-running VW bus and walk several blocks on foot. I reach the Hollywood Cemetery gate and stand alone in the dark. I don't want Cinderella to have the satisfaction of knowing my curiosity has gotten the better of me.

Climbing with great difficulty over a low decorative metal fence, I sneak inside the grounds. I'm tired of all the news about the Confederate soldiers. The way the media plays it, Cinderella is a damn hero, and I'm a shitless creep. If only they knew what my sister is really like.

With my flashlight, I follow a stone path, trying to find the pyramid and crypt where the soldiers from our backyard are buried. This place is like an enormous maze, but the stars are bright and I can make my way, even with overhanging trees and randomly placed benches.

I quiet my breathing when, after an hour of searching, I come upon the site. Shining my flashlight, I can see that the small door to the crypt is slightly ajar. Something or someone is inside. This makes little sense since it is three in the morning. Then I hear a ferocious growl. My body goes taut. That's all I remember.

Voices speak above me, but I cannot respond.

"Best I can figure," a male voice says, "a wolf or rabid dog attacked him. Nearly ripped his throat out."

"Weird, though," says a higher male voice, "because there've been no wolves around here for years."

"Hmp. Maybe a wild dog or a pack of them. Never seen anything like it before. Animal Control will be all over it."

"And look at those puncture wounds on his throat. Lucky he didn't bleed out."

"Hands are mostly gone too. Looks like they were chewed off. Least the paramedics got the bleeding stopped pretty quick. Good thing the night watchman heard him screaming."

"Yeah, thank goodness for Charlie. He's no dummy. He might be old, but he was a medic in the war. To my way of thinking, this poor sap was being pulled *away* from the crypt. Can't make no sense of it. It's like it was a phantom animal. No trace of it to be found. And Old Charlie didn't hear or see nothing of an animal when he found the body."

"Any idea of who the poor guy is?"

"Wallet was in his pocket. Might be related to that woman in the papers—the one that got those soldiers moved here. Same last name, anyway."

"Out of the way, officers," a female voice says. "We've got to get this man into surgery. You can get more information when he comes to."

"You think he'll make it?"

"Probably, but I'm not sure he'll want to."

I can't wake up. A wolfdog attacks me over and over. I can't fight him off. I have no hands.

CHAPTER FIFTY-EIGHT

Susan

The police ask me questions about why my brother might have been in the cemetery in the middle of the night, but I have no answers. They believe me. From what they say, it surprises me Golden Prince is alive.

I'm offered a job at Hollywood Cemetery as a tour guide, which I happily accept, even after Golden Prince's attack. My first day of work is July 1, 1992.

A social worker from the hospital calls me at work since I have no phone at Moon Woman's house. She says that as Golden Prince's next of kin, I should come in and speak with her, but I ask her to tell me the issues over the phone. She informs me that Golden Prince will soon leave the hospital and go to a nursing home.

"Your brother will need help for the rest of his life," she says. "I'm so glad I finally located you. Family is important, and when we move him, you should be there."

"My brother is on his own," I say. "I feel bad he'll never play the piano again, but it won't be me who cares for him."

* * *

I've been living with Moon Woman for several months, and we often talk late into the night. She seems to possess a power of a different kind.

"There are many paths to travel," Moon Woman says one night as we sit on her back porch. "At some point you'll be able to forgive your older brother. It will take time, and it may not be in this lifetime. Regardless, you should be patient with yourself."

"But what if I can't forgive him?"

Moon Woman smiles at me. "Sometimes it's four steps forward, five steps back. Your time will come, and then you'll be set free."

"I hope you're right."

"If you're on a path you shouldn't follow, then you should not stay with it under any condition. Always ask yourself, Does this path have a heart? If it does, it's good and will lead you on a joyful journey. If it doesn't, it's of no use and will either weaken you or cause you misery."

"Being born into my family," I say, "I never knew I had choices, but now I do. I've followed a long path with no heart, and I'm ready to leave it behind. I'm officially changing my name to Susan Divers."

* * *

I'm surprised to run into Luke at a grocery store near Moon Woman's house. I haven't seen him for a few years, but he still looks like a cowboy straight off of *Bonanza*, and more handsome than ever. He tips his hat when he sees me and says, "Howdy, ma'am, it's been a long time."

I don't realize how much I've missed him until I see his twinkling eyes. "Can you come to dinner tonight at my friend's house?" I say. "I'm picking up ingredients to make lasagna. Please say you will!"

"Don't you think you'd better clear it with your friend first?" he says.

"Believe me, she won't mind. In fact, she'll be delighted. Is six all right?"

"Sure. I'd like to catch up on what's been happenin' with you. How 'bout I bring some wine and Budweiser?"

That night, over dinner, we laugh and swap stories. When I talk about Chestnut and the special rides we shared, Luke's eyes light up before a look of sorrow comes over his face. "Those were good times, except for the end. I still feel real bad about that."

"I don't blame you for anything," I say. "You and Chestnut saved my life. And by the way, I should let you know that I've changed my name to Susan Divers."

He smiles. "The name suits you well."

I laugh because it's true.

That night, I do something unusual. I tell Luke about the atrocities that went on in my home. It feels good to unburden my past, especially to a close friend.

Luke becomes a constant in our lives. Moon Woman and I go to the stables and ride with him as often as we can, and he comes for dinner at least twice a week. Savory aromas and plenty of laughter fill those nights.

"You might think about gettin' another horse," Luke says to me one evening after the three of us share a pizza. "I have one in mind for you and one for Moon Woman too. How 'bout y'all come to the stables next Tuesday?"

Moon Woman's horse is a gentle five-year-old gray mare. "I'd like to name her Stardust," Moon Woman says while smiling at Luke. "Her other name doesn't suit her energy, but Stardust does."

My horse, a four-year-old filly, is solid black with white markings. She is more rambunctious than Stardust, and it's love at first sight.

"Her name is Sparkles," Luke says, "although I'll never know why. She has a bit of an attitude, but you can handle her."

I hug his neck. "Where did you get Stardust and Sparkles? They couldn't be more perfect for us."

"Love finds a way," he says with a grin.

I spend as much time at the stables as possible. Being with Sparkles fills my heart with joy. Plus, I want to give Luke and Moon Woman plenty of time to be alone.

On the nights when all of us ride together, I watch love unfold. A beautiful energy surrounds Moon Woman and Luke, and before long, the two most important people in my life become a couple. We are a horse family and I feel blessed.

CHAPTER FIFTY-NINE

Susan

Since I work at the cemetery, I'm able to get permission for my spirit group to be there after hours for paranormal investigations. Our group of five meets once a week. We invite the soldiers and anyone else who might still be earthly bound to go to the light. Often, we see the image of a man with flowing white hair. He wears a general's uniform and brass-rimmed glasses, and he rides a saddled mule. He does not know the war is over, and we've not been able to convince him otherwise. I've learned that spirits cannot be commanded.

After one of our meetings ends, I stroll through the cemetery with Moon Woman and Luke. When the night turns fully dark, Thomas appears and holds my hand while Wolfdog walks beside us. One world has moved on, but for Thomas and me, this one has not.

We all live happily ever after except for...

Golden Prince, who lives in a state-run nursing home for those with no funds. After a few years pass, I visit him there. His Parkinson's has worsened, and he's in a wheelchair. He lifts his head when he sees me. I think I detect a flicker of recognition in his eyes, but it quickly disappears. He has no voice—it was taken on the night of the attack—and his throat bears the scars as proof.

Patricia, the social worker from the homeless shelter, works here now. She recognizes me when I enter the dementia ward.

"Look who's here to see you, Golden Prince," she says. "It's your sister, Susan." She bends down to my brother's eye level. "You must be proud of all the good work she's done in raising awareness of our Civil War soldiers. A real historian she's become. I've read article after article about her and her public speaking engagements and fundraisers. She's a regular celebrity. You must be very proud of her."

"That's kind of you, Patricia," I say. "I'll always be grateful for what you did for Luther."

"He was the kindest man I ever met. He preached from the Bible but was never pushy about it like some are. If he had a sandwich, he'd offer you half, even if he hadn't eaten and was hungry himself.

"Many people loved your brother, myself included. And, oh my, did he have a soft spot for the ladies who worked the corners at night, always watching over them and running off unsavory men who meant to do them harm. He might not have been able to stop the world's oldest profession, but he recognized danger when he saw it and protected his ladies no matter what."

She leaned down to my oldest brother's level again. "Golden Prince, I'm sure you're very proud of your siblings." Then she stood and faced me. "I need to get back to work, but I couldn't resist saying hello. It's great to see you again."

I take a moment to ponder Patricia's words to Golden Prince and wonder if any of them registered with him. I'll never know. He's asleep in his chair. Or faking it. I pull a copy of *Rolling Stone* from my purse and place it on his lap. I look at him one last time.

I won't be coming back.

AUTHOR'S NOTE

"Everything great in the world is created by neurotics. They have composed our masterpieces, but we don't consider what they have cost their creators in sleepless nights, and worst of all, fear of death."

~Marcel Proust

Lured by the seductive call of creativity, I pick up my pen and write, not knowing what kind of journey I am about to embark upon. With this book I venture beyond the safe and ordinary affairs of my life to delve into the darkness of human thoughts and actions. I hold nothing back.

Depression, trauma, hostility, and love are driving forces behind my novels. While working with plot lines and arcs, I allow myself to be caught up in curious but symbiotic relationships, with my characters turning their stories—and mine—into creative expression. I believe that intuitive writers such as myself are blessed and cursed.

I once knew the characters in this book. They were adults when I met them, and they found in me a sympathetic ear. I write about them now as they are no longer in bodies, their lives cut short.

Their stories ingrained in my memory, are highly fictionalized, though the framework of the story is true. The characters actually existed, but the details are drawn from my imagination to add coherence and connectivity. It all begins with the sins of the mother, Anastasia, a horrible person who broke the wings off her babies so they could never fly, and Bastard Man, the father who thought his wife could do no wrong.

Pissant and Cinderella is a terrible Grimm's-like fairy tale. Most children set out on different paths toward rightful destinations, finding their way to happiness with only the occasional ogre or monster. But for Pissant and Cinderella, such is not the case, for their ogres are many. Their paths are slippery, dark, and twisted. Even their detours lead back to the hell of home. Sometimes surviving is all there is.

Millions of people who are victims of sexual degradation and incest often drown their pain in addiction while splitting off into other realities. None of us should be ashamed of where we come from or where we are going, as long as we do our best not to damage ourselves or others.

I hope Pissant and Cinderella know that I am writing this story for them and are smiling. They would want this story told if it helps but one child.

If you gained something from *Pissant and Cinderella*, please consider posting a review on the site of your choice. Reviews are difficult to come by and very much appreciated.

All of my books are available on Amazon, and I love to connect with readers on my Facebook Author Page, so please feel free to visit me there:

www.Facebook.com/LindaKaySimmonsAuthor

HOTLINE RESOURCES

If you recognize abuse in your own life or that of another, please know that help is available. You can check the internet for helpful websites and hotlines, but below you'll find a few trustworthy resources that might give you a start. Help is but a phone call away.

The National Domestic Hotline 800-799-SAFE (7233). Advocates are available 24/7 to discuss your situation and help you identify options to ensure your safety.

www.thesafespace.org: How to stay safe, speak out, and break the cycle of violence.

www.breakthecycle.org: Dating violence and abuse.

www.loveisrespect.org: 1-866-331-9474: A twenty-four-hour confidential hotline that supports teens who are experiencing dating violence. They support the parents of such teens as well.

www.rainn.org 1-800-656-HOPE (4673) Rainn offers free, confidential, secure service that provides help for survivors of rape, abuse, and incest.

The National Suicide Prevention Lifeline is a United States-based network of over 160 crisis centers that provides 24/7 service via a toll-free hotline: 1-800-8255 (TALK). It is available to anyone in suicidal crisis or emotional distress. The caller is routed to their nearest crisis center to receive immediate counseling and local mental health referrals.

WARNING SIGNS OF ABUSE

- Unwanted attention, jokes, mean comments, harassment, or touching that is not okay with you.
- Insulting, demeaning, or shaming you, while alone or in front of other people.
- Being told you don't do anything right.
- Pressuring or forcing you to have sex or perform sexual acts you're not comfortable with.
- Pressuring or insisting you use drugs or alcohol.
- Intimidating you through threatening looks or actions.
- Showing extreme jealousy of your friends or resenting time you spend elsewhere.
- Preventing or discouraging you from spending time with friends, family members, or peers.
- Preventing you from making your own decisions, including about working or attending school.
- Controlling finances in the household without discussion, including taking your money or refusing to provide money for necessary expenses.

- Insulting your parenting or threatening to harm or take away your children or pets.
- Intimidating you with weapons like gun, knives, bats, or mace.

OTHER BOOKS BY

LINDA KAY SIMMONS

Cahas Mountain

Cahas Mountain chronicles the love, heartbreak, and redemption of Rhodessa Rose and Lily, two Appalachian women connected through duplicitous moonshiner Willard Grimes, who offers nothing but a mouthful of sweetness and broken promises.

Filled with big ambitions, Willard courts and weds Rhodessa Rose in the shadows of Cahas Mountain. But his greed takes him into dangerous company as he runs his 'shine and evades the law.

Left alone by her philandering husband, gutsy Rhodessa Rose battles a tuberculosis epidemic—and her desire for the local ʰeriff—in a beautiful story set against the shattering backdrop ᵈd War II and its aftermath. Will Rhodessa Rose rise to the challenge and deny her heart's desire, or will she give in to the lust that tempts her and the curse of moonshine's empty promises?

Lightning Shall Strike

Thaddeus Simpkins, dark master of his household and esteemed elder in the Waters of God Believers Church, rules his family in appalling and unforgivable ways. His younger brother, Joseph, flees with the orphan girl he loves to find a new life away from his intolerable existence under Thaddeus's thumb. When tragedy strikes the young couple, one of them is forced to return to Thaddeus's home.

Meanwhile, questions about lunacy are never far from the mind of Thaddeus's sister, who is painfully aware of her niece's banishment to an asylum. She knows that the niece's punishment is unfair and laced with ignorance, but fighting against it may cost her everything. Will the family ever escape Thaddeus's shadow and find the love that has eluded them for decades?

Lightning Shall Strike pulls at the boundaries of desire and despair, where love stubbornly persists and beauty shines through.

Lamb On A Tombstone

Lamb On A Tombstone is the haunting coming-of-age story of Elton, a shy boy who witnesses his father's sudden death. Left to be raised by his alcoholic mother, Elton tries to cope with his dysfunctional home life and his sensitivities to the dead. His only solace is Aunt Emily—but she has her own set of secrets.

At night, Elton sees the dead emerge from the woods behind his house. Ghost Girl requests his help early on, but others soon follow. Later, stumbling upon a corpse, Elton alerts the authorities and becomes embroiled in the investigation, unaware of his proximity to the murderer.

As time progresses and Elton grows up, he moves closer to a fate he never imagined.

Feel free to contact Linda Kay at:

www.Facebook.com/LindaKaySimmonsAuthor

Made in the USA
Columbia, SC
20 July 2021

Made in the USA
Columbia, SC
20 July 2021